THE L[ORD,]
THE VOW, AND
THE PLAIN JANE

(The Lords of Eton, Book 2)

Bereft of beauty as well as fortune, the exceedingly plain Miss Jane Featherstone has failed to attract any suitor during her three Seasons. Rather than be a burden to her brother and his obnoxious wife, Miss Featherstone vows to accept the first man who asks—even though she's always worshipped a lord who's far above her touch. . .

Lord Slade must marry an heiress in order to honor the deathbed vow he made to his father, and he needs Miss Featherstone's help in wooing her beautiful cousin. After her initial anger, Miss Featherstone agrees to his scheme, telling him she's doing so because she admires his Parliamentary record of humanitarian legislation and his reverence for truth. But the more he's with the two cousins, the more attracted he becomes to Miss Featherstone. What's a man of his word to do? Break a vow to a beloved father— or follow his heart with Miss Featherstone?

Some of the praise for Cheryl Bolen's writing:

"One of the best authors in the Regency romance field today." – *Huntress Reviews*

"Bolen's writing has a certain elegance that lends itself to the era and creates the perfect atmosphere for her enchanting romances." – *RT Book Reviews*

The Counterfeit Countess (Brazen Brides, Book 1)
Daphne du Maurier award finalist for Best Historical Mystery

"This story is full of romance and suspense. . . No one can resist a novel written by Cheryl Bolen. Her writing talents charm all readers. Highly recommended reading! 5 stars!" – *Huntress Reviews*

"Bolen pens a sparkling tale, and readers will adore her feisty heroine, the arrogant, honorable Warwick and a wonderful cast of supporting characters." – *RT Book Reviews*

His Golden Ring (Brazen Brides, Book 2)
"*Golden Ring*...has got to be the most PERFECT Regency Romance I've read this year." – *Huntress Reviews*

Holt Medallion winner for Best Historical, 2006

Lady By Chance (House of Haverstock, Book 1)
Cheryl Bolen has done it again with another sparkling Regency romance. . .Highly recommended – *Happily Ever After*

The Bride Wore Blue (Brides of Bath, Book 1)
Cheryl Bolen returns to the Regency England she knows so well. . .If you love a steamy Regency with a fast pace, be sure to pick up *The Bride Wore Blue.* – *Happily Ever After*

With His Ring (Brides of Bath, Book 2)
"Cheryl Bolen does it again! There is laughter, and the interaction of the characters pulls you right into the book. I look forward to the next in this series." – *RT Book Reviews*

The Bride's Secret (Brides of Bath, Book 3)
*(*originally titled *A Fallen Woman)*
"What we all want from a love story...Don't miss it!"
– *In Print*

To Take This Lord (Brides of Bath, Book 4)
*(*originally titled *An Improper Proposal)*
"Bolen does a wonderful job building simmering sexual tension between her opinionated, outspoken heroine and deliciously tortured, conflicted hero." – *Booklist of the American Library Association*

My Lord Wicked
Winner, International Digital Award for Best Historical Novel of 2011.

With His Lady's Assistance (Regent Mysteries, Book 1)
"A delightful Regency romance with a clever and personable heroine matched with a humble, but intelligent hero. The mystery is nicely done, the romance is enchanting and the secondary characters are enjoyable." – *RT Book Reviews*

Finalist for International Digital Award for Best Historical Novel of 2011.

A Duke Deceived
"*A Duke Deceived* is a gem. If you're a Georgette Heyer fan, if you enjoy the Regency period, if you like a genuinely sensuous love story, pick up this first novel by Cheryl Bolen."
– *Happily Ever After*

Books by Cheryl Bolen

Regency Romance

The Lords of Eton Series
   The Portrait of Lady Wycliff (Book 1)
   The Earl, the Vow, and the Plain Jane (Book 2)
   Last Duke Standing (Book 3 due late 2018)

Brazen Brides Series
   Counterfeit Countess (Book 1)
   His Golden Ring (Book 2)
   Oh What A (Wedding) Night (Book 3)
   Miss Hastings' Excellent London Adventure
      (Book 4)
   A Birmingham Family Christmas (Book 5)

House of Haverstock Series
   Lady by Chance (Book 1)
   Duchess by Mistake (Book2)
   Countess by Coincidence (Book 3)
   Ex-Spinster by Christmas (Book 4)

The Brides of Bath Series:
   The Bride Wore Blue (Book 1)
   With His Ring (Book 2)
   The Bride's Secret (Book 3)
   To Take This Lord (Book 4)
   Love in the Library (Book 5)
   A Christmas in Bath (Book 6)

The Regent Mysteries Series:
   With His Lady's Assistance (Book 1)

A Most Discreet Inquiry (Book 2)
The Theft Before Christmas (Book 3)
An Egyptian Affair (Book 4)

Pride and Prejudice Sequels
  Miss Darcy's New Companion
  Miss Darcy's Secret Love
  The Liberation of Miss de Bourgh

My Lord Wicked
A Duke Deceived

Novellas:
Christmas Brides (3 Regency Novellas)

Inspirational Regency Romance
Marriage of Inconvenience

Romantic Suspense
Texas Heroines in Peril Series:
  Protecting Britannia
  Capitol Offense
  A Cry in the Night
  Murder at Veranda House
Falling for Frederick

American Historical Romance
*A Summer to Remember (*3 American Historical
Romances)

World War II Romance
It Had to be You

DEDICATION

For my cousin Liz Tabb, who will always be
Betty Lou to us.

THE EARL, THE VOW, AND THE PLAIN JANE

(The Lords of Eton, Book 2)

Cheryl Bolen

$\mathcal{C}$hapter 1

As much as Miss Jane Featherstone adored her lovely cousin, Lady Sarah Bertram, she most decidedly disliked riding in Hyde Park with her on this fine May day. Not because of any fault of Lady Sarah's but because of Miss Featherstone's own unpardonable jealousy. Her clandestine envy was positively illogical (and Miss Jane Featherstone had always prided herself on her ability to master the principles of logic).

It wasn't as if any of the Most Eligible Matrimonial Catches would have given a second glance to the exceedingly drab Miss Featherstone were the dazzling Lady Sarah not perched beside her.

In the ten minutes since the maidens' open barouche had passed through the gates into the bustling park, no less than five young men of title, fine looks, and amiability had sputtered their horses to a halt in order to make cakes of themselves over Lady Sarah.

And it was no wonder. Once her cousin was presented to the *ton* at tonight's ball, every Eligible Matrimonial Catch in the entire kingdom would be hurling himself at the beautiful girl. With hair the colour of wheat sparkling in sunshine, a face as flawless and smooth as the finest pearl, and a figure that curved like that of a Roman goddess, Lady Sarah would effortlessly rise to the top of the pack of this season's debutantes.

When it was discovered the titled beauty was possessed of one of the largest fortunes in Britain, there would be no stopping the stampede to Clegg House in Berkley Square.

Owing to the fact the beautiful heiress had not yet been presented, the young oglers could not directly start a conversation with her until Miss Featherstone did them the goodness of facilitating the introductions.

Therefore, Miss Featherstone was—for the first time since her own presentation three years previously—the object of young men's profound felicitations. Once greetings were exchanged, Miss Featherstone had no choice but to introduce these Eligibles to her spectacular companion.

And then Miss Featherstone would quietly fade into the upholstery like gray paint on tin.

Leaving young Lord Averworth worshipfully watching Lady Sarah continue down the park's broad lane, the beauty turned to her cousin, her blue eyes flashing with excitement. "All the young men I've met are exceedingly nice. I cannot wait until tonight."

"I daresay you'll be like a queen holding court."

"You will put me to the blush."

"I assure you, that is not my intent. We wouldn't want any redness to mar your lovely complexion."

Lady Sarah was too honest to feign maidenly modesty. Not a day of her life had passed that her remarkable beauty not been commented upon. "Nor would I. That's why I'm wearing this hideously wide-brimmed bonnet today."

Miss Featherstone shook her head. "Your bonnet is not hideous. Everything you wear bespeaks impeccable taste." Indeed, thought Miss Featherstone, she had never seen a lovelier bonnet. Where most ladies of her acquaintance changed the trim of the bonnets to coordinate with their clothing, Lady Sarah's entire bonnet perfectly matched the pale yellow of her morning gown. Had she the luxury of a different coloured bonnet for each dress?

"Do you really, truly like the gown I shall wear tonight?" Lady Sarah asked.

"I do, though I daresay if you wore a horse blanket you would still be the prettiest girl at the ball."

"You're much too kind, my sweet Jane."

Miss Featherstone sighed. "Would that I could feel more kindly toward Lavinia." She had prayed to no avail that she and her brother's abrasive wife would rub along together better.

Lady Sarah's eyes slitted. "That horrid woman is positively odious! I will never understand how your brother could ever have chosen to marry her."

"Her generous dowry helped." Unfortunately, none of the Featherstones had a . . . well, a *feather* to fly with.

"Then he probably doesn't love her at all. That's the problem when one is possessed of fortune. One never knows if a gentleman is in love with her or her money."

"If he didn't love her when they married, I believe he does love her now, but you need have no fears of fortune hunters," Miss Featherstone assured. "Men would fall horribly in love with you even if you were as poor as . . . well, as poor as me."

"Your lack of fortune does explain why you've

received no offers, for you are possessed of a great many attributes."

Miss Featherstone adjusted the brim of her bonnet to shield her eyes from the blazing sun. "Pray, my dear cousin, enlighten me on these attributes."

"You may not be beautiful like me, but you really are pretty. In a quiet way."

"You obviously have been too much around my Papa."

"That has nothing to do with my opinion, I assure you. I am possessed of good vision. Your face *is* pretty. You are terribly clever. And there is nothing offensive in your figure."

"If one is given to admiring flagpoles." Miss Featherstone nodded at a pair of giggling girls who were strolling by, parasols protecting their fair faces from the sun.

"Many men prefer slender women. Remember, it's women like me—women with generous endowments—who grow portly with age."

That was true. But, then, many men preferred portly women. Look at the Regent himself! Most of the women with whom he'd been romantically linked tended to be as rotund as he.

As they followed along in the procession of fine carriages toward a copse of trees, Miss Featherstone gloried in the sun's warmth, her thoughts snaking around her own abominable envy. There was no reason to feel in competition with Lady Sarah. She loved her cousin, and she knew she could never compete with her in the higher echelons of society.

Miss Featherstone had always understood her own future would be with an equally plain man of no particular distinction. The problem was that not even a plain man of no particular distinction had ever honored Jane Featherstone with an offer of marriage.

Which was a pity. Papa was nearly seventy, and when he was gone, Jane would become the burden aunt in her brother and Lavinia's household—a prospect as unwelcome to Lavinia as it was to Jane.

When their coach neared the Serpentine, she thought she recognized Lord Slade riding alone on a striking black mount. Her back straightened. Her gaze narrowed. And as she realized he was riding toward them, her heartbeat clanged against the walls of her chest.

Since the very day Miss Jane Featherstone had come out of the schoolroom, she had secretly worshipped the man. Long before he succeeded to his title, she had admired his brilliant orations in the House of Commons. Her dear Papa was one of Lord Slade's staunchest allies against the beastly Tories. She had filled a book with newspaper accounts of his lordship and tucked it in a drawer beneath her jewel box.

Not only did she vastly admire his intelligence and political philosophy, but she also thought he was perhaps the most physically appealing man she had ever seen.

Of course, he likely would not remember someone as plain as she. Before he moved up to the House of Lords upon his father's death, he had come to their home often to discuss political reform with her father and their colleagues in the House of Commons.

Because she served as her father's hostess and because her father rather indulged his only daughter, Miss Featherstone had been permitted to join in on those conversations.

As Lord Slade drew nearer, his eyes appreciatively raked over Lady Sarah, then flicked to Jane, and a smile of recognition lighted his tanned face. Dear heavens! The man was going to stop and speak to them. She was quivering so, she doubted she would be able to summon her voice.

Their scarlet-liveried driver pulled up when he saw that Lord Slade had stopped.

"Good afternoon, Miss Featherstone. I see you're also enjoying this fine, sunny day." From his wide shoulders to the squared planes of his face to his casually tossed deep brown hair, the man exuded the most ruggedly handsome masculinity she had ever beheld.

He eschewed the trappings of dandies and dressed in riding clothes with neither shiny top hat nor shiny boots. His buff-coloured breeches stretched over long, muscled legs, and his brown boots would have been more appropriate in the country than here in the middle of London. That he was not a slave to fashion rather endeared him even more to Miss Featherstone.

"Indeed, my lord," she managed, thankful her voice had not betrayed the rattling within her.

He nodded, then his flashing black eyes perused Lady Sarah.

Jane realized he was expecting an introduction to the Incomparable. "Lord Slade, may I present my cousin, Lady Sarah Bertram?"

Lady Sarah bestowed her brilliant smile upon her latest admirer, and they exchanged greetings.

After saying all that was proper, Lord Slade's once again directed his attention at Miss Featherstone. "Then you two are related on your mother's side? Was Lady Mary not sister to the Earl of Clegg?"

Had Miss Featherstone's departed mother—the Lady Mary to whom his lordship had just referred—appeared on this meandering trail, Jane could not have been more stunned. Lord Slade had remembered her mother was the daughter of an earl. "Yes. The Earl of Clegg–who's my mother's brother–is Lady Sarah's father."

"Then you're the granddaughter of George Berkley?" he said to Lady Sarah.

Everyone in the *ton* knew that George Berkley's significant banking fortune had been settled on his first granddaughter, who just happened to be the astonishing creature sitting there in her father's barouche in Hyde Park.

Lady Sarah smiled. "Indeed he was. Did you know him?"

A pity her cousin's lengthy lashes swept down upon her cheeks, Jane thought. Could anyone be more beautiful? Pangs of jealousy spiraled within her. What a beastly pity Jane could never appear to such advantage to his lordship.

"I did not have that pleasure, but he was banker to my father—who greatly admired him."

"As did I," said Lady Sarah, her voice lifting into the sweetest possible tones.

"Tell me, my lady, why is it I have not yet met you before?"

"I have not been presented. Well, actually I was presented to the queen yesterday."

"And she comes out tonight," Jane added. "Will you attend the ball at Spencer House, my lord?"

His crooked smile returned. "You may be assured I will." He doffed an invisible cap, favored them with his infectious smile, and took his leave.

When he was out of earshot, Jane turned to her cousin. "What did you think of Lord Slade?"

Lady Sarah shrugged. "I didn't think about him one way or the other. I will own, I was prepared to dislike him excessively. Papa, you know, detests the man's radical ways in Parliament. He's always grumbling about Lord Slade."

"Then I daresay Uncle grumbles about Papa, too, for he and Lord Slade are rather two peas in a pod."

"It's no secret, of course, that Papa and your father do not agree on matters of government, but your papa is family, so Papa never maligns him."

"Gentlemen are much nicer than ladies." How could Lady Sarah not be in awe over his Sublime Lordship? Had the dust kicking up from hooves clouded her vision?

"You're right. Papa never speaks ill of Lavinia, and you must own *everyone* speaks ill of Lavinia."

Jane nodded absently. Incomprehensibly, Lady Sarah still had displayed no great admiration for Lord Slade. "Did you not find Lord Slade uncommonly handsome?"

Lady Sarah shrugged again. "He's . . . older than what I normally find attractive."

"He's not even thirty!"

"And I'm not quite eighteen!"

"Then you're attracted to young men closer to eighteen?" *How very peculiar.*

Lady Sarah nodded. "Up to my brother's age."

Lord Harry was two and twenty. "But most men of that age—unless they've had the good fortune to succeed—are not in a financial position to offer for a wife- - -" Miss Featherstone thwacked her forehead. "Such consideration, though, is unnecessary to a lady of large fortune."

"Indeed. I can wed whomever I choose." She gave a stupendous smile and pronounced, "I shall be wed by September."

"If that's what you want, I'm certain you will. Why the hurry?"

"I adore the idea of having my own house. Wouldn't it be wondrous to marry a man with a family castle? With my fortune I could decorate it whatever way I choose. And I love children. I see myself surrounded by beautiful little blond daughters. "

"What of sons? Or a husband?"

Lady Sarah Bertram scrunched up her perfect nose. "I suppose my husband will expect me to give him an heir, even though I'm not overly fond of little boys. Of course, I do long for a husband."

"Perhaps you'll meet him tonight."

***

"I beg that your lordship stand still," Lipton said to Lord Slade.

With a deep sigh, Slade straightened his neck and peered into his full-length looking glass. His man labored over tying the cravat Lipton had spent a goodly amount of time ironing. It was far more important to Lipton than to Slade that his master present an admirable appearance.

If Slade were at liberty to please only himself, he would not be standing there. He would not be going to the Spencers' ball at all. And he would not be preparing to offer up himself like the day's catch at Billingsgate fish market.

But the earl was not at liberty to please himself. He was now head of the household. He must think of the others. Buying David's colours had nearly cleaned out his limited funds, and he would have to put off the girls' come-out at least another year.

Since the exchange had decimated his father's blunt, there simply wasn't enough money despite all his measures to economize. He'd leased the London house and presently let rooms at a respectable address. He'd sold the costly carriage and three of the four horses it necessitated. He and his siblings occupied but one wing of crumbling Dunvale Castle, which could now be run with a fourth as many servants as when the old earl had been alive.

His gaze followed Lipton's expert manipulations, and he frowned deeply. Why had he made that wretched Vow, the Vow that would irrevocably alter the course of his life?

How much happier he'd been before he succeeded. Until he saw Miss Featherstone that afternoon, he'd almost forgotten how greatly he'd enjoyed those lively Whig discussions at dinners presided over by that extraordinary young woman's father. Why, there had been more intellect within those modest walls than in all of the House of Lords.

The door to his dressing room eased open, and his brother strode in. Slade thought his brother—Captain David St. John—cut a handsome figure in his Life Guards' uniform. Women would be sure to swoon over him tonight. They always did.

"I thought Lipton was dicked in the nob when he told me you were going to the ball at Lord Spencer's tonight." David looked at Slade as if the elder brother were mentally deficient. "Didn't know debutantes were your thing."

"Heretofore, they haven't been." Slade's lips set into a grim line.

David smacked his forehead. "Oh, yes. The

Vow."

Lord Slade nodded almost imperceptivity, saw that Lipton had not left even a speck of lint on his freshly pressed jacket of fine black worsted, and was satisfied with his appearance. Nothing too colourful for him. Black and white was just fine. "Shall we go?" he said to David.

Chapter 2

It was impossible for Miss Featherstone to feel even the merest pang of jealousy when she gazed upon her cousin that night. How could one feel anything but admiration when beholding a Da Vinci for the first time? Every facet of Lady Sarah's beauty was a thing to stare at for the very pleasure it gave.

What a vision of innocence she presented with her youth, her milky, unblemished skin, and her modest dress of fine white muslin. Her golden locks swept back from the perfection of her unpainted face, and a small necklace of pearls clustered in gold completed the picture of simple elegance.

Jane had been struck by such remarkable loveliness only once before. She recalled how she had drunk in the beauty of her eldest niece the first time she saw her. Bess was six months old with creamy skin and wisps of fine blond hair when Jane first beheld her. She thought she had never seen anything more lovely. (And, uncharitably, she wondered how Lavinia could have given birth to anything so beautiful.)

It was rather the same with Lady Sarah this evening. As lovely as she was, though, she clung to Jane like a frightened toddler to her nurse as the young ladies squeezed through the doorway and into Lord Spencer's overcrowded ballroom.

"I am so very happy you have been through this before." Lady Sarah had virtually shouted at Jane in order to be heard over the roar of at least a hundred voices and the drowned-out strains of orchestra music. "You will be able to tell me how to act."

Owing to the crush of people, Miss Featherstone did not immediately reply. They pushed themselves against the flow of bodies damp from the rigors of dancing. Miss Featherstone automatically went to her preferred corner—as far from the orchestra as possible. "You need no instruction from me," Jane said when they reached their destination. "Just smile and act as you do at any country assembly. Forget that this ballroom is adorned with gilt and silken draperies and pretend it's the council hall in Stockton-on-Wye."

Lady Sarah exhaled. "An excellent plan! You're always so terribly clever."

Part of Lady Sarah's apprehension, Jane knew, stemmed from the fact she was acquainted with very few of the two or three hundred people in Lord and Lady Spencer's bulging mansion. She was not on friendly terms with a single one of the other girls being presented with her that evening.

Miss Featherstone patted her cousin's gloved arm. "By the end of the night, you'll feel old friends with half of those in this chamber, and the callers will start pouring into Clegg House at midday tomorrow."

"I pray you're right." Lady Sarah watched the finely dressed dancers. "Have you ever tripped and fallen when you danced?"

"No, nor have I ever witnessed such an occurrence."

"I declare, that is most reassuring."

Before Lady Sarah had the opportunity to sit in one of the unoccupied chairs lining the wall, an army of admirers swooped down upon her, and she was swept onto the dance floor.

In her corner, Miss Featherstone was saved from humiliating isolation by the companionship of Miss Ophelia Lambeth. The unfortunate Miss Lambeth was even more plain than Jane. Miss Lambeth wasn't so much plain as she was . . . well, there was no other word for it. She was *homely*.

She was taller than most men and had the misfortune of possessing a nose that would not have been so out of proportion had it been on an eighty-year-old man of large stature instead of upon Miss Lambeth's narrow face.

"There is one recommendation for spending the better part of a ball seated," Miss Featherstone said to Miss Lambeth.

"You must reveal it to me so I can tell my mother."

Miss Featherstone smiled wickedly. "We need never worry about wearing holes in our costly dancing slippers."

Miss Lambeth's satin-covered toe pointed out from beneath her pink skirts. "Indeed. These have held me in good stead these five seasons past." Not even a hint of bitterness tinged the good-natured young woman's voice.

Lest Miss Featherstone be a hopeless wallflower, her cousin, Lord Harry, did her the goodness of standing up with her not once but twice. How fortunate was the girl who would one day catch the considerate young man.

Later that evening, Jane stiffened when she

saw Lavinia enter the room, pause, and scan the ballroom until she saw Jane. Then, glaring, she moved across the floor to where Jane and Miss Lambeth sat. Without being invited to do so, she sat beside her sister-in-law. "I must have a word with you."

Jane forced a smile. "About what, dearest?"

"About the company you keep."

Surely she was not going to disparage poor Miss Lambeth in the lady's presence. "Pray, to whom could you be referring?"

"That cousin of yours!"

Since Jane had recently danced with him, she asked, "Lord Harry?"

"Of course not! I refer to his sister."

"Is there something about Lady Sarah to which you object?"

A prodigiously menacing expression on her face, Lavinia said, "It's not *her* that's the problem, it's you."

"Enlighten me, please."

"I wouldn't be concerned were I not so excessively fond of you, dear Sister," Lavinia began, "but it simply won't do for you to be seen with anyone as beautiful as that cousin of yours! Why, you'll never snare a husband."

"You must own I've failed to catch one these three years past. Have you not given up hope?"

"I pray every day you will find a man who's as wonderful a husband to you as your brother is to me."

Jane had no doubt the self-absorbed Lavinia did indeed offer up such a prayer. It was no secret she could not abide the idea of being saddled with Jane for the rest of her life.

Lavinia's gaze whisked over Jane, and she

shook her head sadly. "May I offer you another suggestion? Something for your own good?"

"Pray, do."

"Why do you not get your hair shorn? Long tresses are sadly outdated, and it's my belief the shorter style would show you to better advantage."

"Would shorter hair render me as pretty as Lady Sarah?" It was most difficult for Jane to withhold her facetious smile.

"Honestly, Jane, I thought you were more intelligent than that! You will never even hold a candle to your cousin."

Lavinia's bejeweled hand wound into her own curly black tresses, revealing a handful of previously hidden gray strands. "I daresay had I shorn my hair as it is now I'd have been able to attract at least an earl when I came out."

Fifteen years had passed since Lavinia had come out. Was she still embellishing her own unremarkable entré into society? Fashionable hair could hardly have compensated for Lavinia's bulging eyes and crooked teeth, Jane thought— most uncharitably. "No earl could have been as fine as the man who won your hand."

"Of course, you're right." Lavinia sighed, then shrugged. "We'll have to wait three more years for our Bess to come out. We do have our hopes. With her beauty, a duke is not out of the question."

"I pray that you don't fill my niece's heads with such thoughts. We would not want her disappointed if she fails to make an aristocratic marriage."

"You sound exactly like Robert."

Jane's brother was exceedingly wise. Even if he had chosen Lavinia for a wife.

"I have decided to sit for a spell with you,"

Lavinia continued, "even though I heartily disapprove of the way you plop yourself down in the back corner, acknowledging to the entire *ton* that no man could possibly desire you for a partner."

"Shh." Jane's eyes indicated Miss Lambeth. "Would you wish I draw attention to my ineligibility from center front?"

"You need not announce your ineligibility at all. You may not possess fortune or beauty, but you *are* the granddaughter of an earl. That should count for something."

The very mention of her husband's connection to so lofty an aristocrat evoked a smug smile on Lavinia's face. She was loathe to acknowledge that her own grandfather had been but a brewer.

Jane shrugged. "Such inducements have not succeeded, I'm afraid." Secretly, Jane was congratulating herself that a man shallow enough to select a bride based on her grandfather's rank was *not* a man she would wish to marry.

Lavinia paid her no attention. "Will you look at Miss Bullen? Her dress looks like something a deranged gypsy would wear!"

"Shh! I fear the dancers will hear you." Jane was powerless not to cast her glance to the dance floor where Miss Bullen, dressed in a pink gown edged with three rows of purple ruffles, was gracelessly dancing down the longway with her partner, blissfully unaware of how truly hideous her dress was. It really wasn't fair that she could merit a partner when Jane couldn't.

"It's far too noisy for anyone to pay the least heed to what I'm saying."

Then Lavinia did something even more unpardonable. She pointed at a portly young woman standing in the opposite doorway. "I don't care if Annabelle Sommers does have five hundred a year, the poor girl doesn't have a prayer of getting a husband."

Miss Featherstone was mortified. "I beg that you not point, Lavinia. And, pray, please speak in a softer voice, though I'd as lief you not speak ill of anyone." She unfurled her hand-painted fan. It was getting excessively hot. And she wasn't even dancing! Lady Sarah's dress had to be drenched.

Lavinia and Jane both watched Lady Sarah. Jane had not had the opportunity to speak to Jane since the first dance of the night. The young men were nearly at dagger points with each other, vying to stand up with the beautiful heiress, to procure ratafia for her, or just to get close enough to hear the melodious sound of her voice.

If one could judge from the expression on Lady Sarah's face, she was most decidedly enjoying her first ball.

"I understand the betting books at White's are full of Lady Sarah," Lavinia said. "Wagers are in on who she will marry as well as what date an announcement will be made."

Miss Featherstone was not listening. Her attention had been captured by her friend Lady Wycliff. What a change had come over her since she married! She'd not only been close to a man-hater in those days before she fell in love with Lord Wycliff, but she'd also eschewed events such as this where she was presently dancing with an admiring man who was not her husband. Their eyes caught, and Louisa Wycliff's lighted with recognition.

As soon as the set came to an end, she fairly flew across the dance floor to greet Jane. Louisa

Wycliff rivaled Lady Sarah in beauty. She had always been beautiful, but since she had married Lord Wycliff, she'd become even lovelier. The somberness that had marked her previously had been replaced with a gentle look of perpetual happiness. Especially when she was speaking to her husband.

And the clothing she had acquired since her marriage! No one could dress more beautifully. Tonight she wore an exquisite gown of pale blue muslin that was no thicker than a sheet of foolscap. Its bodice and train were embroidered with tiny white flowers, and a crown of white flowers adorned her silky blond hair.

"I did not know you attended such functions, Miss Featherstone."

Jane smiled. "Nor did I know you did."

Lady Wycliff rolled her eyes. "Lord Spencer is very important in government, and my dear Harry wishes to court his favor." She shrugged. "I, too, have decided that to help Harry's political aspirations, I must make every effort to act as if I were born to these affairs--which you know I was not! I've decided to let his mother guide me."

"But I thought Lady Wycliff died some years ago."

"Yes. More than a decade--long before I knew Harry, but the woman was perfection. I want to do everything she did so Harry will think me the perfect wife."

A pretty blond girl tapped on her ladyship's shoulder. She turned around and smiled. "You didn't tell me you were coming here tonight!"

"I decided to when Edward told me you'd be here."

Lady Wycliff turned back to Jane. "You

remember my sister, Mrs. Coke?"

A strong resemblance existed between the two, despite an age disparity of nearly ten years. The younger sister had married Lord Wycliff's cousin the same time Lord and Lady Wycliff married. "Yes, of course, she's one of our Tuesday ladies. How lovely you look tonight, Mrs. Coke."

"It's lovely to see you here, Miss Featherstone. I hate to steal Louisa away, but I promised Lady Soames I'd introduce her to my sister."

As Jane watched, the pretty sisters wove in and out of the crush toward the door. Then she saw him. Lord Slade entered the ballroom. He was accompanied by a handsome military officer who Jane recognized as his younger brother. Though his brother immediately latched on to an eager dance partner, Lord Slade moved into the crowd, then surveyed the room with a look of bored disdain. Owing to his height, his head of dark brown hair towered over a sea of paler heads.

As he came closer, she was able to observe him in full, glorious length. This night he did not defy fashion but dressed perfectly in black, save for the snowy white linen of his shirt and cravat that tied simply beneath his square chin and matched the white in his teeth.

Regrettably, his gaze followed Lady Sarah as she stood gracefully in the longway, her hands linked to the gentlemen beside her while she watched the couple move between the two lines of dancers.

"I declare," Lavinia said, rising, "Lady Spencer is unattended. I must go speak to her."

"Your cousin is exceedingly popular," Miss Lambeth said, half yawning as she spoke.

"One as lovely as she will not be long on the

Marriage Mart."

"I daresay you're right." With a sigh, Miss Lambeth rose. "It's time to fetch Mama. She tires so easily at these events." With that, the docile Miss Lambeth excused herself.

Jane did so hate her friend to leave for then she would be quite alone in her corner. Her gaze followed Miss Lambeth as she clomped around the perimeter of the dance floor.

"Good evening, Miss Featherstone."

She spun around, looked up, and saw the handsome man not two feet away, looking down upon her.

"Good evening to you, my lord." Oh, dear, was he going to ask her to stand up with him? Her irrepressible pulse began to gallop.

"I beg that you allow me to sit by you."

She was almost relieved he was *not* going to ask her to dance. If any lady ever did fall down during the execution of dance steps, it would have been Miss Featherstone in her nervousness over dancing with the man she so worshipped. "I am honored, my lord."

Tonight his dress was as elegant as the afternoon's had been careless. Both, Jane thought, were magnificent. Every aspect of his grooming spoke of cleanliness. Miss Featherstone could even smell his soap as he sat next to her.

"Tell me, Miss Featherstone, are you still so passionately interested in government?"

"I am, my lord."

"I've very much missed those stimulating dinners at your home."

"As we've missed you. I daresay Papa misses you even more as a colleague in the House of Commons."

"Just because I've moved to the upper chamber does not mean I would not still be gratified to be included among your father's guests."

"I feel certain I can speak for Papa when I say our door will always be open to you, my lord. As a matter of fact, we're a hosting a small dinner tomorrow night for some of Papa's fellow Whigs. We would be exceedingly honored if you would come."

"It's I who would be honored to attend." His black eyes met hers. "I'm honored to be invited. My political philosophy did not suddenly change because I succeeded. I will always be a Whig."

She remembered anew why she had begun to so admire him in the first place. Above all, he had always been a man of principle and high moral values. "You must own, most of your fellow lords oppose everything you have always promulgated."

"That will never stop me from continuing to work toward reform."

"I am very happy to hear that, though, of course, I already have surmised as much."

"Because you still stay well informed over measures in both houses?"

She gave a little laugh. "It's one of my hobbies." *Obsession, really.* But no maiden in search of a mate should ever admit to being a bluestocking.

He favored her with his disarming grin. "And the other one, as I recall, is executing wonderful architectural drawings."

The man's phenomenal memory continued to astonish her. "I don't know that I'd call them wonderful, but I love to draw classical buildings."

"One day I shall have to entice you to make a rendering of Dunvale Castle."

"It would take no enticement at all, my lord.

Doing so would give me great pleasure."

His long legs stretched out in front of him, and it appeared he was content to stay right there with her. Upon reflection, she realized Lord Slade seldom attended these gatherings, even though he would be considered one of the Most Eligible Matrimonial Catches in the kingdom. "Do you not like to dance, Lord Slade?"

"Dancing and *liking* to dance are two entirely different matters."

Her eyes twinkled. "Then it appears we are in agreement upon another matter." If he did not wish to dance, though, why was here?

"It's most gratifying to be in the company of one who shares so many of my own ideals," he said. "In fact, Miss Featherstone, I came here to tonight expressly to see you."

"Me, my lord?"

He nodded. "Indeed. There is a very important question I must ask you."

$\mathcal{C}$hapter 3

He'd always thought of Miss Featherstone as a girl, but as he sat beside her in the noisy ballroom it suddenly occurred to him she was no longer a girl. She had grown into a young woman. How shocking that she had not married. What was she now? One or two and twenty? The young men must be fools if they hadn't snatched her up. He knew nothing to her detriment and a great deal to her credit.

Though her appearance did not dazzle like her cousin's, Miss Featherstone possessed a delicate prettiness that could easily be overlooked. Perhaps it was her slenderness that made him find her delicate—like a twig that could easily snap. He watched her long, graceful fingers restore a jeweled pin into her long, wavy, soft brown hair.

Even her dress of pale blue evoked delicacy. He noted that its bodice was cut a bit higher than other women's. Most ladies who did so wished to conceal their overabundance of bosom; Miss Featherstone likely did so to conceal her lack of bosom. Yet despite her boy-like chest, the lady was unquestionably feminine.

"What, my lord, is the question you wished to ask me?" She peered up at him with lichen green eyes, and he noticed the little row of freckles that sprinkled across her nose.

He regarded her with amusement. "The first thing I must ask is if you're still reform mad."

"Oh, most decidedly," she said.

"And which particular reform do you see as being the most urgent?"

"It's difficult for me to say, especially since you are . . ."

"An aristocrat?"

She nodded, and he was reminded of how young and sweet she had looked opposite the dinner table from her doting father during those lively dinners. Yet she had served as his hostess most capably, despite that she could not have been much more than fourteen when she started.

"May I try to guess?" he asked.

She nodded again, barely suppressing a smile.

"You object to the fact that so many seats in the House of Commons are controlled by a handful of powerful peers."

"It really is an outrage."

"I agree."

She favored him with a smile, and he was once again struck by the realization that she was no longer that precocious girl, but a full-fledged young woman.

"Worst of all," she continued, "is the rotten boroughs. They are a painful reminder of how antiquated our system of government is."

"I agree. Neither house is representative of the people we are supposedly serving."

"Like the thousands of people in Birmingham who have no representation at all?"

He nodded. "While a pasture in Cornwall does?"

"Exactly!"

"It's my pleasure to tell you that we now have a new ally in the House of Lords."

"Besides yourself?"

He nodded. "Yes, my dear friend Lord Wycliff."

Her mouth gaped open. "I did not know you were friends! His wife has long been one of my closest friends."

"Then that must mean she's one of your bluestocking friends."

"Indeed. Our group has always met at her house--even before she married his lordship."

"I know the house well. Wycliff and I have been close friends since we were young lads at Eton." She regarded him with narrowed eyes. "I declare, my lord, I believe you used your persuasive abilities to encourage him to take his seat in the House of Lords just so that he could support our cause."

His eyes sparkled. *Our cause.* "Between that lovely wife of his and me, poor Wycliff had no choice."

At that very moment he witnessed Wycliff emerging from the card room to stand and survey the large ballroom that was near bursting with finely dressed members of the *ton.* When his gaze alighted on Slade's, a smile of recognition brightened his face, and then he strode toward them.

Slade introduced Miss Featherstone to his friend.

"I beg, Miss Featherstone," Wycliff said, "that you will forgive me if I lapse and address my old friend as Sinjin. It's what we all called him for a great many years."

She nodded. "At Eton. Actually, I've heard him addressed as such before. When he was in the House of Commons."

"Her father . . ." Slade started to say before

Wycliff cut him off.

"Must be Harold Featherstone. I am a great admirer of him."

"When I had the pleasure of serving in the House of Commons," Slade said to his friend, "I was privileged to attend dinners at the Featherstone house. A gathering of more well-formed minds I've never attended."

"My wife thinks we should start emulating such gatherings at Wycliff House." Wycliff eyed Miss Featherstone. "Your father would most certainly be welcome."

Slade chuckled. "Miss Featherstone is every bit as astute on political matters as her brilliant father. I daresay if you invite him, you must invite her."

Wycliff screwed up his face in thought. "Now that I think on it, I do believe my wife is already acquainted with Miss Featherstone."

"Indeed, my lord," that young lady responded. "I've had the honor of attending her Tuesday gatherings for several years. In fact, I was introduced to you there before you married."

He thwacked his head. "I do remember. It was the only time I ever attended one of Louisa's Tuesday sessions." His voice softened. "It was the luckiest day of my life. It was the day I met my wife."

Wycliff was still a sappy newlywed who was madly in love with his countess. How fortunate he was to be able to marry for love, something Slade would never be permitted to do. He was very happy that his old friend had found such happiness in marriage. Wycliff had been raised in an extremely close family of three. Just him and a pair of adoring parents. When they died, he'd been lost and bitter, but all that was behind him now that he'd found a wife he worshipped and who worshipped him in return.

While Wycliff had been standing there, his eye kept following his pretty wife as she gracefully danced across the ballroom, and when the set was finished, he excused himself and claimed her for the next set.

Slade returned his full attention to Miss Featherstone. "May I say how much I'm looking forward to renewing those dinner conversations with the erudite Miss Featherstone? And your father, of course." He used to marvel at how well read and well informed she was—and that was before she'd officially entered society.

Not many men he knew were possessed of as much knowledge as was crammed into her youthful head. "Until I saw you in the park today I'd forgotten how very much I enjoyed those evenings I spent at your home. How long has it been?"

She shrugged. "I expect we haven't seen you since your father's last, grave illness."

"Then it's been nearly four years. You've grown from a girl to a woman in that time. I should be honored to dine at your house tomorrow night. Will your cousin be there?"

A puzzled look passed over her face. "Lord Harry?"

How stupid of him to have expected the most popular debutante in London to choose to spend an evening discussing political reform at her uncle's modest home. "Actually, I was referring to Lady Sarah, but I realize now how unlikely that would be."

Miss Featherstone's gaze swept to the dancing

floor where Lady Sarah was presently standing up with Lord Slade's dashing brother. "I believe my cousin will be dancing blisters on her feet for the next several nights."

"You will not accompany her to all the fetes?"

"It was important for me to be with her this first night, but I believe she will be more than capable of handling herself from here on out."

"It just seemed to me this afternoon in the park that your cousin rather deferred to you."

"How perceptive you are. We are as close as sisters—neither of us having a sister—and, owing to the fact that I'm three years her elder, Lady Sarah has always rather looked to me for guidance." She paused, casting a quick glance at her elegant cousin. "But as you can see, in a single night the pupil has surpassed the teacher."

He shook his head. "I beg to differ. Were Lady Sarah to sit at your father's table tomorrow night, your acumen of politics and literature would likely leave her sadly in your dust."

"You're much too kind."

"I'm honest."

"I have noticed that about you. Sometimes your honesty hinders your . . ."

Silence stretched between them while Miss Featherstone was obviously searching for a non-offensive comment.

Then he understood. "You refer, of course, to my effectiveness in Parliament?" The lady was too gracious to malign him, but he was well aware of the many times his truthful tongue had gotten the better of him on the floor of the House of Lords. And in the House of Commons before that.

To this day, Lord Haygood refused to speak to him, and he couldn't blame the man. After all, he'd referred to the Tory—on the floor of the House of Lords—as a "bloated parasite gorging on riches won by his long-ago ancestor."

"Exactly." Her eyes flashed with mirth.

"You certainly are your father's girl. A pity you weren't a male. We could use you in Parliament."

"Papa's always lamented that my brother Robert did not choose to stand for office. Of course, it *is* very expensive. It's understandable his wife would wish to funnel funds elsewhere. Not all of us are as wealthy as George Berkley was."

Money! That's why Miss Featherstone had not married. None of the Featherstones had a feather to fly with. "How well I know about that. In fact," he cleared his throat. He hated like the devil what he was about to do, but it was his duty. "In fact, that brings up the question I wished to ask you tonight."

Her thin, nicely arched brows rose.

"I intend to court your cousin, and I would be grateful if you could lubricate my way into her intimate circle. While such a request might be onerous to you, I assure you I have the best intentions."

This was devilishly difficult for him. All afternoon he'd practiced what he was going to say, and now he recited his points like a schoolboy racing through his memorized Chaucer. "Allow me to appeal to your altruism, Miss Featherstone. I remember well how that bleeding heart of yours bent and cracked over any misfortune to orphans or to others who've been oppressed, and were I to marry Lady Sarah, I vow that I will put her money to humanitarian use."

There! He had finished his plea. Had he just

proposed to the heiress he'd met but once, he could not have felt more nervous than he did at this moment.

Miss Featherstone did not respond. Her soft brown lashes lowered, and she appeared to be examining the fan gripped tightly in her fingers.

From the turmoil he read in her expression, he already knew the answer. In his nine and twenty years, Jack St. John, the fourth Earl of Slade, had never been more humiliated.

In the same way that her brilliant father never spoke rashly but gathered his composure while rationalizing a situation before commenting, Miss Featherstone must be carefully arranging her rejection before speaking.

Finally, she looked up from the fan, and squarely met his gaze. "It pains me to have to turn you down, my lord, but you must realize the selection of a husband is something my cousin must do with no help from me—or anyone." Then she stood, looking down at him.

He'd never felt so small.

"I must assume your reacquainting yourself with me was for this nefarious purpose, and I won't expect you at dinner tomorrow." She spun away.

He lunged from his chair and snatched her gloved arm. "I *will* be at your house tomorrow."

"Very well." She whirled back and left the chamber.

He hated what the Vow had made him become.

* * *

She raced down two flights of stairs, and on the ground level she found the French doors leading out onto the terrace which gave onto Green Park. Speeding past gathered couples who were merrily chatting, she rushed out into the vast blackness of the park. She had to get away. She couldn't let anyone see her in such a distressed state.

Sweet heavens! She had almost burst into tears in front of Lord Slade. All because she had been so ridiculously stupid as to have thought the man was going to ask for *her* hand! How could she have been such an imbecile?

He *had* said he'd come to the ball expressly to see her. Then he flattered her prettily and said he had a question to ask her. What was a lady to think?

Now she felt like a rug he'd wiped his shoes upon.

Equally disappointing was how far her respect for him had plummeted. She had never thought the noble lord would sink to marrying for fortune, and that is exactly what he intended to do. As pretty as Lady Sarah was, Jane knew the man could not have formed a deep attachment to her after one brief meeting. Why, he hadn't even danced with her!

How could he wish to pledge the rest of his life to a woman for the sole reason that he wanted control of her wealth? His single act—or more precisely, his mercenary intention—had stripped from him every commendable trait she'd ever admired. How could she have been so wrong about his character?

Her stride fast and furious, she paced in the park, her fists clenched tight, her eyes stinging. Her thoughts in a black swirl, she was startled when, at length, buttery squares of light seemed to burst through the darkness. Houses. How far had she gone? The pounding in her heart had by now returned to normal. She finally forced herself to stop and get her bearings. It took her a minute to realize she'd reached Buckingham House. She hadn't gone so terribly far, after all. It had gotten beastly chilly. She rubbed her arms, lamenting she'd not stopped for her shawl.

She turned around and headed back. It was so dark she could barely see where she was placing her satin slippers, but she knew she must hurry. Her reputation could be ruined if she did not immediately return to Spencer House. Besides, it was almost time for supper, and she was uncommonly hungry.

When she returned to the lantern-lighted terrace she was relieved the others had gone inside, obviously for supper. No one would witness her indiscretion. She climbed the steps and entered the house a great deal more calm than when she'd left.

The late-night supper at these balls, though, always posed a problem, owing to the fact a lady must wait until a gentleman honored her by asking to escort her to the table. It was rather embarrassing not to be paired. Often, her dear cousin, Lord Harry, would do her the honor. Would he forgo the opportunity to escort a lovely debutante in order to spare his cousin?

She reached the corridor at the same time as Lord Slade's brother. The brothers' appearances were very similar. Both were tall and possessed of dark chocolate-coloured hair, and there was also a strong resemblance in their faces. Lord Slade, though, was a great deal more muscular than his brother. Some might say Lord Slade was too large. It was true, she must admit, the younger brother's build with his exceedingly trim waist and wide shoulders would be considered perfection, while

Lord Slade might be considered just a *large man.*

His gaze met hers, and a smile flashed across his handsome face. "Miss Featherstone, is it not?"

"Indeed, Mr. St. John, or should I call you. . ." She looked at the various medals pinned onto his scarlet military jacket. "I know I should be able to know your rank, but I'm sadly ignorant of such matters."

He chuckled. "From the one and only time I had the pleasure of your company, I would have to say the word *ignorant* could never be applicable to you." He gave a courtly bow. "I am now known as Captain St. John."

Other couples around them began to pair up for supper. "Would you do me the goodness of allowing me to escort you to dinner?" he asked.

She only barely suppressed a huge sigh of relief as she placed her hand in his. "I would be honored, Captain."

She was happy to find Lady Sarah and Freddie Whey sitting across the table from her. "Do you know my cousin, Lady Sarah?" Jane asked the captain as he assisted in scooting in her chair.

He smiled at the lady in question. "I am beholden to Sir William for making me known to the lady. How do you do again, my lady?"

Lady Sarah fluttered her lengthy lashes. "Very well, thank you, Captain."

"I should think you must be welcoming the opportunity to sit," Jane said to her cousin. "You've danced every single set."

"Oh, la! I enjoy dancing vastly." Lady Sarah turned to her partner. "Are you acquainted with my cousin, Miss Featherstone?"

Freddie Whey, who was a year younger than Jane, nodded. "Yes, I've had that pleasure."

"How do you do, Mr. Whey?" Jane said by way of greeting.

She was very sure his response was all that was proper, but for the life of her, she could not hear it.

As the long table filled, the drone of more than a hundred voices made communicating across the table excessively difficult--in addition to being a breach of etiquette.

She then directed her attention on the officer beside her. "I must own, Captain, I was astonished you remembered me," she said over cold, diced mutton sprigged with fresh parsley. "You must have been just a boy when we met."

"Indeed. It was five years ago, when I was seventeen."

So he was a year older than she. "However would you remember that?"

"Because Jack did not deem me mature enough for dinners at Featherstone House until I was seventeen, and the following year I was off to India." He tossed back a sip of his champagne. "I must own, I was most curious to meet the girl Jack was always telling me about."

She gave him a quizzing look.

"You, Miss Featherstone. Jack would lament that I was not more diligent in my studies. 'Miss Featherstone is younger than you, and she knows everything,' he would tell me. So, of course, I was most impatient to meet this remarkable girl he was always blathering about."

Some of her depression lifted away, like a gray cloud to reveal a blue sky. Lord Slade had actually admired her! "Then you must have been very disappointed when you did make my acquaintance."

"Not at all. I still remember what was being discussed that night. Penal reform. I shall always remember your insistence there should be a hierarchy of offenses, that the punishment for poaching should not be the same as for murdering. That sort of thing."

"If your memory is that remarkable, then you must have been a far better student than you say."

He vigorously shook his head. "That's why I'm a soldier. "

She was struck by how much he looked like his brother. Only his brother was far more grave. "Your facial expressions are so much like your brother's, except that you're a jollier version."

"It's no wonder. I have the good fortune to be the second son."

Her brows hiked. "You prefer being a younger son? No title? No fortune?"

He laughed out loud. "There is no fortune. There's nothing but a crumbling castle, a pile of debts, and a pack of siblings who have to be provided for. And if all that wasn't enough crushing responsibility, poor Jack was pressured into making a deathbed vow to our father that I don't think he'll ever be able to keep. And to know Jack is to know he has always prided himself on his truthfulness."

"Indeed." She wanted to ask what the Vow was, but it really wasn't her concern. Lord Slade was nothing to her. The Vow between him and his dying father was a deeply personal matter. Nevertheless, she was consumed with curiosity.

"You understand, I'm telling you this only because I know you and my brother are on some terms of intimacy," he said.

If he thought that, perhaps he might tell her what The Vow was. Of course, she had no right to ask. Absolutely no right. And she most certainly was *not* on any terms of intimacy with Lord Slade! She hadn't even seen him in nearly four years.

But he had actually praised her to his brother! Such knowledge had the power to make her feel as if she were walking on clouds. All these years she had believed he couldn't possibly notice anyone as plain as she (no matter how pretty her father told her she was). All these years she had rather fancied she blended in with the wallpaper. And all these years Lord Slade--who'd been Lord Jack St. John then--had actually been aware of her! She was exceedingly flattered.

Being aware of her, though, was nothing like actually being attracted to her. He was an earl, after all. His looks and title could win any woman's heart. A man who could have any woman he chose would never settle for a drab thing like her.

Of course, tonight he had destroyed her high opinion of him.

"Oh, yes," she said. "I've always been a great admirer of your brother. I'm sorry to learn that he's under an obligation he is unable to fulfill. Pray, is there any way I can help?" Perhaps now he would tell her more about the mysterious Vow.

He shook his head sadly. "Not unless you had a fortune."

She shrugged. "You know what they say about us Featherstones?"

"Indeed." He gave her a sheepish grin. "You don't have a feather to fly with."

They both laughed.

"The pity of it is, the money poor Jack needs

will be impossible to raise. Unless he . . .well, there's nothing for it but to . . ." He looked around to make sure no one was listening, and then he lowered his voice. "marry a considerable heiress."

She could stand it no longer. Now he was blathering, and he hadn't got to the point! "Why must he possess a considerable fortune? Pray, what *was* the Vow?"

He looked taken aback. "Did I not say?"

"No, you did not."

"Well, then, Papa asked Jack to save Dunvale Castle, to bring it back to glory. You must know the old pile is crumbling."

"Actually, I've never been to Dunvale."

"There's little to see anymore. We're reduced to occupying but two floors in one wing. It's really ghastly. The turrets have tumbled, and the keep has kaput."

She felt ashamed of herself for giggling over so serious a problem, but Captain St. John was most entertaining. "How long has the castle been in your family?"

"That's the pity of it. Since the Conquest."

"Oh, dear. I do see why your father was so keen to preserve it."

"But his request, you must own, was beastly unfair to Jack."

"Without question."

"There are also the girls."

"You mean your younger sisters?"

"Yes."

"How many of them are there?"

"Three."

"I see. Lord Slade must present them *and* dower them?"

He nodded. "In time, I think he'll be able to

manage that. He's very clever about economizing, and he has no vices like gaming and. . .well, you know the sorts of things a lot of bloods do."

Her nose wrinkled with distaste. "Indeed."

"He's bought my commission, so that at least is behind him."

"One down. Three to go."

"Exactly," he said, smiling. "Allow me to pour your wine." He filled her fine crystal glass with a French wine. Jane supposed Lord Spencer had filled his cellars back in '02 after the Treaty of Amiens had provided a temporary respite from war with France.

Though she had been ravishingly hungry, her appetite vanished. How terribly she had misjudged Lord Slade. She should have known the man who had always championed the unfortunate would be just the sort to sacrifice his own happiness in order to help others. Not that marrying Lady Sarah would exactly be sacrificing his happiness. Lady Sarah was all any man could want in a wife.

But somehow she did not think Lady Sarah was the sort of wife Lord Slade would have selected, had he free choice.

She looked up and down the table and all around the room, searching for Lord Slade, but he was not there. "Where is your brother?"

"He's gone. Must have left about an hour ago."

"Without dancing?"

Captain St. John shrugged. "Now that you mention it, I don't remember seeing him on the ballroom floor all night. Of course, balls have never been to Jack's taste."

She need not ask why he had chosen to come tonight. "What about you, Captain? Do you like to attend balls?"

He glanced across the table at Lady Sarah. "Very much." His gaze returned to Jane. "It's gratifying to find so many lovely ladies all in the same room."

She could well believe he was quite the ladies' man. In temperament, the brothers were as dissimilar as she and Lady Sarah.

She pushed away her untouched plate of sweetmeats. Her heart went out to poor Lord Slade, who was so weighed down caring for his family and worrying about that wretched Vow. Not that there was anything she could do to help him. It wasn't as if she could order her cousin to fall in love with him.

Could she even try to assist him in his quest?

What a heartbreaking choice she had to make.

$\mathcal{C}$hapter 4

"Oh, dearest, I just remembered we'll have to add one more plate," Mr. Featherstone said to his daughter.

Jane drew a long breath, gritted her teeth, then whirled around to face her father. "Now you remember to tell me—when the guests should be here in less than ten minutes." She stormed to the butler-less butler's pantry to fetch one more plate, her father's shuffling gait trying to catch up with her.

"What's one more?" he asked, shrugging.

She grabbed another gilt-edged dish and hastened back to the dining room. "It's not just one more plate, it's one more mouth to feed. Do not dare to take a second helping of turbot!"

He threw up his arms. "Why are you in such a dust-up today, love? You act as if we're entertaining the king himself."

"I am *not* in a dust-up. I'm trying to be my father's competent hostess." Her voice softened as she met his gaze. "Pray, Papa, who is this unexpected guest?" All she'd been able to think of all afternoon was one specific guest. *Lord Slade.*

"A fellow by the name of Cecil Poppinbotham."

"I'm certain I would remember that name. Are you sure he's in Parliament?"

"Not yet. Wilhampton says that Poppinbotham's keen to stand for the Plymouth seat and that he's got significant funds to finance it."

"His own money?" She rearranged the plates on one side of the table in order to squeeze in one more.

Her father carried another chair to the overcrowded table. "Yes. The man's a printer. Made a fortune publishing penny pamphlets."

"I don't think I've read penny political pamphlets." Miss Featherstone stood back and admired her work. Neither the table nor the dining room was more than a quarter the size of her uncle's, Lord Clegg's, yet the elegance of Mama's delicate plate and the baroque silver epergne could not be surpassed at any of London's finest homes.

"Oh, they're not political. They're religious. Moral tales and the like."

"Then I daresay I've purchased a few," she said. "But why does the gentleman wish to come here?"

"Apparently he wants to represent Whigs."

A rapping sounded at the door, but of course her father did not hear it—though he would never admit he was losing his hearing. "Do go and get the door, Papa. Our first guest must have come." Her thoughts flitted to Lord Slade. One who was used to a house full of servants was probably not accustomed to residents answering their own doors.

She recounted the place settings, then scurried down the backstairs to the kitchen to see if Mrs. Nolan and the half-day cook should need her.

By the time she strolled into the drawing room several minutes later, each of the invited guests had assembled. Including Lord Slade.

All the gentlemen accorded her the courtesy of standing when she entered the chamber. One second of recognition, then her gender would be completely forgotten when the discussions began.

Mr. Fortorney, a longtime colleague of her father's, addressed the devastatingly handsome Lord Slade. "May I say how honored we are that you still embrace us, my lord?"Lord Slade's gaze flicked to Jane for the briefest second before he answered. "The honor is entirely mine. I had not realized until I spoke with Miss Featherstone yesterday how very much I had missed these stimulating talks." His voice lowered. "How much I miss serving in the House of Commons."

"Oh, come now, Slade," her father said, "you cannot be sorry to have inherited a title *and* Dunvale Castle."

His lordship gave a bitter laugh. "While I have some affinity for the family name and for Dunvale, I have never admired the English system of aristocracy."

"Why is that?" Mr. Goldfinch asked.

"I find men admirable for the deeds they've done—not for actions of long-ago ancestors. When I'm on my deathbed, I don't want to be remembered as the fourth Earl of Slade. I wish to be remembered for any good I may have done for my fellow man."

"Dare I offer an opposing comment at my first foray into the Whig inner circle?"

All eyes turned to the speaker, the newcomer, Mr. Cecil Poppinbotham.

Jane took this opportunity to study the printer. She judged his age to be forty for his slickened black hair—most fashionably styled—was threaded with gray. His rather gaunt face was at odds with the jauntiness of his dress. In fact, his whole manner of dress was that of a much younger man, perhaps a dandy on his first visit to Town.

The white stripe that ran vertically along his rust-coloured pantaloons matched the linen of his cravat, but there all coordination ended. His waistcoat was of lime green, his jacket a deep plum, and his shoes a peculiar shade of gray. There was a certain crispness about his clothing that attested to its newness, and the tailoring seemed very fine, indeed. No doubt, he had spared no expense in his quest to be a popinjay.

Instead of thinking ill of him, though, Jane determined to be extra solicitous toward the poor fish out of water. She also realized the uninitiated like him might believe members of the House of Commons were truly common, when in actuality the majority consisted of peer's younger sons and brothers and others sponsored by powerful aristocrats.

"Please do, Mr. Poppinbotham," her father said.

"I believe it's unEnglish to lambast our system of aristocracy."

Mr. Arthur nodded. "Daresay, I agree with you!"

Mr. Poppinbotham preened. "People who oppose our system of peerage are cut from the same cloth as those who guillotine kings, meaning no offense to you, your lordship."

Lord Slade merely nodded at the newcomer, a sliver of a smile tilting at the corners of his mouth. Miss Featherstone ran an appreciative eye over the earl. The somberness of the muted browns he wore certainly did not compete with the newcomer's foppish clothing.

The drawing room door opened, and everyone eyed the gray-haired Mrs. Nolan. The matronly housekeeper had kept everything in the

Featherstone house running smoothly for more years than Jane had existed. "Dinner's on the table," she announced, then she returned to the kitchen.

As they moved into the dining room, Jane watched Mr. Poppinbotham with amusement as he paused in front of the gilt-framed mirror, screwed up his mouth into a self-satisfied smile, and pet his greasy hair in the same loving way one pets a favored dog. Even as he walked away, he could not quite relinquish his reflective view— until he bumped into the door jamb.

Besides her father and herself, seven others gathered around the rectangular table and began to fill their plates from steaming bowls that spread across the starchy white cloth.

After the diners had filled their plates, Mr. Featherstone said, "Tell me, Mr. Poppinbotham, what made you decide to stand for Plymouth?"

That he had not quite finished chewing his Brussels sprouts did not stop Mr. Poppinbotham from immediately responding. "I had the honor of meeting his grace, the Duke of Hawthorne, last month at the opening of a Sunday school he sponsored. At a small reception afterward, he was saying he hoped a Whig would stand for Plymouth, but it would take a man of means. By the manner in which he observed the quality of my dress, it was obvious he was referring to me. Though I'm not given to boasting, I had to, in all truthfulness, admit to his grace that I am perhaps the most prosperous prin . . ., er, publisher in the kingdom."

"So you announced your candidacy then and there?" Lord Slade asked.

Mr. Poppinbotham nodded. "I felt it my duty to

give of myself for my country."

"Very commendable," said Jane's kindly father before turning to the earl. "You, my lord, are certainly facing an uphill battle in the House of Lords with your support of labor unions." His gaze flicked to Jane. "What was it Lord Symthington said last week?"

"If he had to increase wages for the colliers in his mines," Jane said, rolling her eyes, "it would force him to close them. And, of course, everyone knows Lord Symthington's mines have been exceedingly prosperous."

"Indeed," Lord Slade said, "in the past year alone he's purchased a yacht large enough for the Royal Navy and a castle in Ireland that's larger than his castle in Scotland."

"He spouts much the same thing as Lord Bingley said about his prodigious stables," Mr. Goldfinch said with a chuckle.

"Yes," Lord Slade added, a gleam in his black eyes. "If all the grooms were to unionize, he'd have to sell off the finest horseflesh in the kingdom. It does seem to my colleagues that if the citizenry were given decent wages, it would run the entire country into the ground."

"I had the good fortune to view Lord Bingley's stables," Mr. Poppinbotham interjected.

Lord Slade's brows lifted. "Then you enjoy the races at Newmarket?"

"No. No." Mr. Poppinbotham vigorously shook his head. "Never been to Newmarket in my life. I neither gamble nor ride."

"I expect your pr . . ., publishing concerns keep you enormously busy," Jane said.

"Indeed they do, Miss Featherstone."

"Tell me, Mr. Poppinbotham, does Hannah

More write for you?" Mr. Featherstone asked.

"I have had the honor of publishing some of her tracts."

Lord Slade cast a glance down the table at Mr. Poppinbotham. "They must sell exceedingly well."

"Allow me to say I wish I had three of her." Mr. Poppinbotham helped himself to a second serving of turbot, leaving the serving dish empty of everything save the buttery French sauce.

"How many are employed by your publishing company, Mr. Poppinbotham?" Lord Slade asked.

The printer puckered his lips, peered at the ceiling, and mumbled numbers before responding. "I employ a dozen printers, and of course there are the writers, who you might say are the backbone of the business. Then there are the lads who . . .distribute our work. That amount varies considerably. I'd say there are a couple of hundred of them."

"There has been talk of a printers' union," Jane said.

Mr. Poppinbotham's brows lowered. "Yes, I've heard."

"Surely a generous man like yourself," Mr. Featherstone said, "a man who feels compelled to give to his country would not object to the unionization of the printers who work for him."

The printer flicked a glance at Jane before answering. "No, of course not, though my men are already paid a decent wage."

"Very commendable." Mr. Featherstone smiled. "Returning to Mrs. More, I met her once. A most righteous woman. What a pity her sympathies are so firmly with the Tories."

Mr. Poppinbotham's mouth gaped open. "'Pon my word, I did not know that!"

"Like all Tories, she no doubt has a reverence for the monarchy," Lord Slade said.

"Even for mad kings," Mr. Goldfinch said with a laugh.

Jane frowned. "I beg that you not disparage our unfortunate king."

"While I'm no admirer of monarchies, I would never wish either our king or our Regent ill," Mr. Goldfinch defended.

"It's not as if they have power such as the Bourbons enjoyed—and squandered." Lord Slade's gaze swept across the table. "Thankfully our Parliament holds the most power."

Mr. Featherstone nodded. "And controls the Civil List."

Jane smiled to herself, recalling how the government trimmed some of the extravagant requests in the Regent's last Civil List.

"Since you don't approve of the peerage system," Mr. Poppinbotham said to Lord Slade, "does that mean you'd be happy to do away with the monarchy?"

"I'd be no happier abolishing the monarchy than I'd be tearing down my family home, Dunvale Castle. We English have a great respect for tradition."

Mr. Goldfinch attempted to steer the conversation to a neutral subject. "Miss Featherstone, I read in this morning's newspaper of your kinswoman."

Jane's brows lifted. "Lady Sarah?"

Mr. Goldfinch nodded. "It appears she's expected to be the Season's most sought-after prize."

"I cannot imagine anyone else could be possessed of all the attributes that have been bestowed upon my cousin." Jane's gaze flicked to Lord Slade, whose lids were downcast.

"Pray, Miss Featherstone," Mr. Poppinbotham said, "how are you related to Lady Sarah?"

"My mother, Lady Mary, was sister to the present earl, Lady Sarah's father."

"Lady Mary's father was, of course, the previous earl," Mr. Fortorney said.

"And I must say I do have a great reverence for Monmouth Hall, where my mother grew up." Jane smiled just thinking of the stately old home nestled among the gentle hills of the Peak District.

Dinner conversation returned to politics, and Jane took the opportunity to study Lord Slade. He possessed as many attributes as Lady Sarah, though their qualities were in different areas. While he lacked a fortune like her cousin's, his knowledge vastly exceeded hers. Together, they would complement one another and would make a spectacular couple.

Jane had slept little the night before. Her dilemma had kept her awake. Before she made a false step, she had to be certain a union between his lordship and her cousin was in the best interest of both. Then she realized no one would ever take a step if they waited for assurances about the future. Only fools could think themselves certain of the future.

At the end of the evening as the gentlemen began to leave, she escorted Mr. Poppinbotham to the entry hall, and he held her hand a few seconds longer than necessary. "I have business in St. Albans tomorrow, but I beg that you allow me to call on you the day after tomorrow, Miss Featherstone," Mr. Poppinbotham said.

So surprised was she over his interest in her, it

took her a few seconds to realize what he meant. *The man means to court me.* He was as far from Lord Slade as a workhouse was to a palace. Just as far removed as she was from Lady Sarah. With a sinking heart, she knew how she had to reply. "Certainly, Mr. Poppinbotham."

His step seemed lighter as he moved to the door.

Lord Slade left next. His brows had been lowered as he watched Mr. Poppinbotham leave, but when he faced Jane, he was all smiles.

Since the others were not near, she said, "I have a matter I'd like to discuss with you tomorrow, my lord."

"Then I beg that you'll allow me to collect you for a walk in the park."

It was then that she realized he no longer possessed a carriage. Two days ago he'd been riding a horse. Tomorrow he'd walk. "Very well, my lord."

***

Miss Jane Featherstone felt like an imposter as she strolled beside Lord Slade. She was not a Pretty Young Thing with whom men-- except for Mr. Poppinbotham--chose to drive or walk through Hyde Park. Never in her one and twenty years had a man so honored her. And it wasn't as if his lordship had singled her out for particular attentions. Her lovely cousin should be sitting in her place.

But if Jane's plan was successful, the *ton* would soon know that it was only a matter of time before Lady Sarah would become Lady Slade.

How very, very fortunate Lady Sarah was, Jane thought, trying to suppress bitterness over her own absence of attractions.

She felt small walking beside this tower of a man. Small and utterly feminine. That's how unquestionably masculine Lord Slade was.

They were deep into the park and had exchanged all the usual pleasantries before he asked her why she had desired a private word with him.

***

He had dreaded this meeting with Miss Featherstone. Ever since the night of the ball, he'd been unable to purge his feelings of shame. Miss Featherstone understandably would think him a fortune hunter, and for some reason it bothered him that he'd sunk so low in Miss Featherstone's esteem. Even though it was done all the time, there was nothing admirable in a man who wed for riches.

She had calculated to bring up her *private* conversation when no others were nearby.

"I have been thinking of the request you made of me the night of the debutantes' ball," she began. His glance flicked to her serious profile. In the daylight the freckles dusting her perfect nose were much more visible than they were at night. She looked more like the girl he'd remembered so fondly than the young woman she'd become.

He frowned. "Must you bring up something which shames me?"

"My dear Lord Slade, you have no reason to be ashamed. You cannot have failed to notice no less than a dozen men have been dancing attendance upon my cousin. And why should they not? She's beautiful, she comes from one of the best families, and she happens to be a considerable heiress."

She was no longer angry with him for scheming to marry an heiress? He straightened, took his eyes off the lane, and stared at Miss Featherstone. "From your actions the other night, it was apparent that you found my interest in Lady Sarah to be. . .*mercenary.*"

"Then I must ask your forgiveness."

"It's I who should be asking for your forgiveness. We both know my interest in your cousin was prompted for reasons that were not the most noble."

Her face whipped to within inches from his. Her mossy green eyes held his. "How can you say it's not noble to want to save a castle that's been in your family since the Conquest? Or that it's not noble to wish to dower your young sisters?"

He abruptly stopped and faced her. "How do you know these things?"

"Your brother did me the kindness of escorting me to dinner after you left Lord Spencer's the other night, and thinking that you and I were on some terms of intimacy, he told me of the Vow."

He sucked in his breath. Neither he nor she spoke for a moment, then she finally said, "I have always admired you, my lord, and I believe of all the men in London you would make the finest husband for my dear cousin."

They came abreast of a passing phaeton and nodded to the passengers. "I am not worthy of your confidence."

"You are a truthful man, are you not?"

"Of course!"

"Then I don't believe you would express feelings of affection toward Lady Sarah unless you were telling the truth. Am I not right?"

"You are right."

"Therefore, I have decided to see that you have the opportunity to win her affections—but only if you give me your word that you will never lie to her."

"You know I would never tell a falsehood."

"That means that the only way you will offer for her hand is *after* you can truthfully tell her she owns your heart."

Love had never entered into his calculations, never been part of his plan. An heir often did not have the right to actually marry for love. An heir had a duty.

How could he possibly know if he could fall in love with the heiress? There was the fact she was lovely. Very lovely. As he thought about what Miss Featherstone said, he realized she had not told him not to offer for Lady Sarah, but just not to offer for the lady until such time he could truthfully tell her he loved her.

Surely he could fall in love with the lady.

While he'd never thought to marry for love, he had always thought that once he was married, he would fall in love with the woman who shared his life and bore his children. And, of course, he would never be unfaithful to the woman with whom he'd been joined to in matrimony.

"So, if I give you my word I would not offer for her until I can offer my love, you will help me woo her?"

"I will."

How would he ever be able to thank Miss Featherstone? Instead of making him feel like a fortune hunter, she tried to make him feel noble. He turned and offered her a smile. "I cannot tell you how honored I am that you have found me admirable. May I ask why?"

"Was it not you who said last night that you want to be remembered for any good deeds you may have done for your fellow man?"

His head inclined, he shrugged.

"I have observed your actions in Parliament since the day you stepped on the floor of the House of Commons." Her voice softened. "I know you're an honorable man."

He kept his eyes ahead. They were approaching Rotten Row, where dozens of conveyances trailed one another. "I thank you."

"Do not hitch all your dreams to the scheme, my lord. It's possible my cousin will favor another of her many suitors over you."

"I am well aware of that."

"Be assured I will sing your praises."

"I am destitute of words to express my gratitude."

She gave him a warm smile. "Now, we must decide on a plan."

$\mathcal{C}$hapter 5

"What a lovely surprise seeing you here this morning," Lady Sarah said as she turned away from her dressing table and studied Cousin Jane.

Miss Featherstone was incapable of removing her gaze from the perfection of Lady Sarah. This morning her beautiful cousin wore a simple dress of sprigged muslin, its tiny flowers matching the blue in her eyes. Her maid had just finished dressing her fashionably short, silky blonde hair. No picture in *Ackermann's Repository* had ever been able to capture a young woman even half as elegant as Lady Sarah.

"I presume the loveliest debutante in all of England is readying to present herself before a bevy of admirers paying a morning call."

"You are, as always, so exceedingly perceptive, Jane. Please say you will join me."

"That's precisely why I've come. What better place to find a room full of eligible men? Not that any of them would ever look at me when you're such a feast for the eyes."

Lady Sarah sighed. "I never thought I'd say this, but it gets terribly tedious being the object of young men's devotion."

"I can see that the proliferation of posies, the perpetual paying of compliments, and the odes written on your beauty could indeed get very tiresome, very fast."

"Perhaps you can latch on to one of my castoffs." Realizing she had just all but insulted her cousin, Lady Sarah leapt toward Jane, holding out her hands. "Pray, forgive me, my dearest cousin. It was most uncharitable of me to say such a thing."

"I've told you countless times to never apologize for saying something which is true."

"You are too dear." Sarah took a last glance in the mirror and started for the door. "One of my suitors, Mr. Mannington, told me at the Vanes' ball last night that he saw you in the park with Lord Slade yesterday afternoon. I must own, I was surprised."

"He's very far above my touch, but we are friends of long standing. He came to dinner at our house the previous night and dazzled everyone at the table with his brilliance."

They left the lady's bedchamber and began descending the majestic staircase of Clegg House. "It's a most fortunate young woman who wins Lord Slade's hand in marriage," Miss Featherstone continued, "for he is possessed of so many admirable qualities. There are his good looks and his position in the House of Lords, and his deep affection for his siblings."

Lady Sarah giggled. "You, my dear cousin, have just described half the men who will be calling on me today!"

In the Earl of Clegg's drawing room, every seat was filled with young men, most of whom were bearing flowers for the earl's lovely daughter. All of them stood when the two young ladies entered the large chamber furnished in dark mahoganies and emerald silk and adorned with paintings by Italian masters as well as a Gainsborough of the present

Lady Clegg as a younger woman with lightly powdered hair.

Presently, that lady, whose hair was now lightly gray without artificial help, sat on a settee in the center of the chamber, smugly satisfied over her daughter's spectacular success.

But it was not that lady who drew Miss Featherstone's attention. Her glance whisked first to Lord Slade. She had known she would find him in the gathering of morning callers, but she was surprised to see that he had come with his brother.

Those two gentlemen quickly offered their chairs to the female cousins.

Seated, Miss Featherstone surveyed the almost all-male gathering. She counted three and twenty young men.

And she realized Lady Sarah had been correct about half of them sharing Lord Slade's attributes of rank, good looks, and amiability, though Miss Featherstone did not think any of them as handsome as Lord Slade or his fine looking brother. And she knew none of them could match him intellectually.

A pity his lordship – unlike the other callers – had not thought to bring flowers to Lady Sarah.

One by one the others filed before the beautiful heiress, presenting her with bouquets and praising her great beauty.

Lady Clegg summoned a footman and instructed him to find vases of water for all the flowers.

"I have searched every flower seller in London," the Viscount Pennington declared as he presented Lady Sarah a single iris, "to find a flower to match the colour of your beautiful eyes."

Did the man not realize irises were *not* blue?

The somewhat portly Mr. Raikes came to stand before the beauty and unfolded a sheet of velum. "Allow me to present you a poem in praise of your beauty, Lady Sarah. I will not take the time at present to read it to you, but I pray you will do so when we take our leave."

"Oh, most certainly, Mr. Raikes. How very kind of you." Lady Sarah barely finished addressing Mr. Raikes when Lord Fordwich came to bow before her, offering a posy of pastel flowers gathered in lace.

"Allow me to say how honored I am to pay tribute to your great beauty, my dear lady."

Miss Featherstone now understood how tedious such adoration could be. For the first time since she had been presented, Miss Featherstone was grateful she did not possess astonishing beauty. She particularly did not ever want to be in the position where she would have to disappoint a lovelorn suitor.

Once all the offerings had been bestowed, the gentlemen began to converse. Would Lady Sarah be at the Rivertons' rout? How had she enjoyed the ball at Lord Spencer's?

The Viscount Fitzherbert asked her if she would join him for a ride in the park that afternoon. Before responding to him, she turned to Jane. "Will you be riding in the park this afternoon, my dear cousin?"

"As a matter of fact I shall." This was a first for Miss Featherstone. Two days in a row she would be escorted to the park by gentlemen. Two different gentlemen–one of whom was very far above her own touch.

"Who will you be riding with?" Lady Sarah

asked.

"Mr. Poppinbotham."

Lady Sarah's brows plunged. "Have I met him?"

"I don't believe so. He's seeking Papa's advice because he means to stand for Parliament."

Lord Slade spoke for the first time since he'd offered the ladies his chair. "I had the pleasure of meeting the gentleman at Miss Featherstone's house this week."

"I understand you're interested in Whig politics, Lord Slade?" Lady Sarah said.

"Very."

The beauty frowned. "Papa is a Tory."

"I have many friends who are Tories," his lordship said.

Lady Sarah's attention returned to the young man who had asked her to ride with him later that day. "How very kind of you to ask, Lord Fitzherbert. Perhaps we can join up with my cousin and her Mr. Poppinbotham."

"He's not my Mr. Poppinbotham!"

Lord Slade addressed the beauty. "A trip to the park certainly does not mean the couples are exclusive to one another." His bitter glance fell first to Viscount Fitzherbert, and then he smiled at Miss Featherstone. "Take me and Miss Featherstone, for example."

"Yes," Lady Sarah interjected, "you accompanied her to the park yesterday, and you are only good friends."

"Almost as a brother and sister," said Lord Slade, his sly glance falling on Lord Fitzherbert.

Though she knew his words true and knew that a plain Jane like her could never aspire to captivate a man as lofty as Lord Slade, his words stung. *Brother and sister.*

***

That afternoon Mr. Poppinbotham came to claim Miss Featherstone exactly at four of the clock. He was dressed in what he undoubtedly considered fashionable afternoon dress for a gentleman of means, but his ideas of fashion and Miss Featherstone's were two entirely different matters.

She could find nothing to dislike in his light gray pantaloons. In fact, they were obviously cut by a master tailor. His waistcoat of purple silk spotted with lavender was a bit more bold than Miss Featherstone would have preferred, and the profusion of knots in his exceedingly large cravat was too overdone for her taste, which veered toward the plain. Like her.

A scarlet coat completed his dress. As one who had studied art, Miss Featherstone understood that all his colours were from the same families, which was admirable. At least he hadn't paired pumpkin with pink. But, still, she could not admire his style.

His equipage was another matter altogether. In this opulent display, Mr. Poppinbotham had put his considerable funds to good effect. All four of the matched bays had been hitched to the gentleman's very fine open barouche, and a driver in lime livery sat up on the box.

"What a very fine carriage this is," she told him as he assisted her onto the rolled leather seat.

A smile of satisfaction lifted his sagging cheeks. "It bloody well ought to be. Set me back four-hundred guineas--not counting the horses which were very dear. Very dear indeed."

She searched her brain, but Miss Featherstone

could not recall anyone of her acquaintance ever disclosing what they paid for something. It simply wasn't done.

Once they entered the gates of Hyde Park, where a queue of equipages funneled inward, such a fine carriage could not go unnoticed. Miss Featherstone was just vain enough to be flattered that a gentleman obviously meant to call attention to his connection with her.

And she did not think he considered them *brother* and *sister*.

When he had called on her, his eye had appreciatively swept over her from the tip of her bonnet and down the length of her soft pink pelisse. "You are the very picture of loveliness today, Miss Featherstone," he had told her. Perhaps some men did admire flag-pole figures.

As she sat beside him, she took the opportunity to discreetly study his person. Though his face and limbs were slender, the man was possessed of a large, round stomach. Certainly nothing like Lord Slade.

She had no right to be comparing the two men. She, certainly, was no Lady Sarah, either in beauty, rank, or fortune. She was bereft of all three. Therefore, she should be grateful to any man who paid her court.

Papa was almost seventy and not in the best of health. Did she really want to be the unwanted maiden aunt in Lavinia's home once Papa was gone?

She flashed a smile at Mr. Poppinbotham. "How did your trip go yesterday?"

"Very profitable."

Is money the only thing the man ever thinks of? "Well, it's nice to have you back in London. You must have sway with the weather gods." Her gaze whisked up at the blue, cloudless sky.

"Couldn't have asked for a finer day."

As they drove along, Miss Featherstone nodded to several lone riders with whom she was acquainted, and she extended greetings to several couples perched on phaetons. That many of those she addressed bore titles obviously impressed Mr. Poppinbotham.

"I envy you your contacts. You are invited into these aristocrats' homes?"

What a silly question! "I suppose I have invitations for events every day of the week at homes of the nobility, but I'm not terribly interested in balls and assemblies."

"What of the venerable Almack's? Have you ever been fortunate enough to wrangle a voucher?"

She laughed out loud. "My first two seasons, I had a subscription there. I chose not to this year because I am not particularly enamored of dancing. Had I need to go there, I daresay I could procure a voucher from my friend Lady Cowper, one of the patronesses." She smiled at him. "Tell me, Mr. Poppinbotham, do you enjoy dancing?"

"Sadly, I must own that when I was a younger man I was too busy making my fortune to go about to assemblies."

"Then you've never learned to dance?"

He shook his head vigorously. "Oh, no, no! I took lessons all of last year. Cost me twenty quid, but when he was finished, my dancing master proclaimed me fit for Almack's."

So he wants to "wrangle" an invitation. Should she try to facilitate it? After a short deliberation, she said, "Should you like me to get you a voucher, Mr. Poppinbotham?"

His dark eyes brightened. She had to admit the man was possessed of very fine eyes. "I would be ever so grateful, but I should not want to go without you, Miss Featherstone."

Because he would know no one. Not a single person. "Would you be available next Wednesday?"

"For something as august as the opportunity to attend Almack's, nothing could be more important. How good of you to ask, my dear Miss Featherstone." He favored her with a broad smile.

In the distance she saw that Lord Fitzherbert was steering his phaeton toward them, looking as proud as a barnyard rooster who'd just sired a peacock, that peacock being Miss Featherstone's lovely cousin.

When they came fully abreast of Mr. Poppinbotham's barouche, Miss Featherstone presented her escort to the viscount and her cousin, and the viscount offered to turn around and ride abreast of them so the cousins could speak freely to one another.

"Fine cattle you've got there, Poppingham," Lord Fitzherbert said.

Mr. Poppinbotham's eyes flashed with good humor. "It's Poppinbotham, your kind lordship. How good of your lordship to notice my horses. I don't mind telling you it was no easy matter finding four so well matched."

The viscount lifted a brow. "You get them at Tattersall's?"

"Indeed I did. I always say nothing but the best. 'Tis my motto. Nothing but the best for Cecil Poppinbotham."

As it turned out, the two men were closest to one another, and they began to discuss conveyances – with Miss Featherstone's escort prompt to disclose his barouche alone cost over four hundred quid.

Not being particularly interested in vehicles, the cousins began to chat. "Another ball for you tonight?" Miss Featherstone asked.

"No. I had but one invitation, and Mama said it would not do me credit to go to the Mortons'."

"Dear love," Miss Featherstone advised, "it's best not to mention people by specific names with such a comment."

"As always, you are right, dear Jane. I wish you could accompany me everywhere."

"It's a great pity our interests are so dissimilar. I adore politics; you are sadly ignorant of such affairs. And I'm a hopeless wallflower while you are the Season's reigning queen. I really would love to spend more time with you, pet, especially since we're both in London. Might I persuade you to come to our house tonight? Papa's having one of his Whig dinners."

"I don't suppose my papa would mind since it's at Uncle's house." Lady Sarah eyed her cousin's escort. "Will Mr. Poppingbottom be there?"

"Poppinbotham. And, yes, he will."

Lady Sarah took that opportunity to stare at her cousin's suitor.

Twice while Miss Featherstone was conversing with her cousin, she heard Mr. Poppinbotham say, "When I get in Parliament."

She would hear more on that subject that evening.

$\mathcal{C}$hapter 6

Lord Slade surveyed the modest drawing room in Mr. Featherstone's house with great satisfaction. There was no other place he would rather be. How he had missed the stimulating conversation of Mr. Featherstone, his brilliant daughter, and his former colleagues in the House of Commons. Featherstone had a knack for assembling around him men who were great thinkers. There were on this evening, though, two exceptions.

Why did Featherstone permit that Poppinbotham buffoon to pollute their gatherings? The man's understanding of the legislative issues of the day was completely lacking – which could tend to explain Featherstone's willingness to take the printer under his wing.

The other exception, Lord Slade looked upon far more favorably. For dear Miss Featherstone had contrived to persuade her beautiful cousin to honor them with her presence this evening. Since it had gotten progressively chillier throughout the day, Lady Sarah wore a gown of soft blue velvet, presenting a picture of complete loveliness. It was difficult not to stare at her. Not in all the years he'd been in London had he ever seen a prettier debutante. And she possessed a fortune, too.

A pity he must compete with such a sea of admirers. At least he had a leg up tonight.

Despite Lady Sarah's dazzling beauty, he found his attention more readily bestowed upon her plainer cousin, perhaps because she made so many contributions to the conversation.

"I must admit to great admiration for the American system of government," Miss Featherstone said when the topic turned to Catholic emancipation. "I believe a society which promotes religious freedom to be a far superior one to ours."

"Did you not also tell me you admired the way the Americans set up representation in the two house chambers?" Slade asked.

She looked up at him and smiled. "How good of you to remember."

As she continued on her theme of obstacles in the way of equalizing representation in the British lower chamber, he was struck by the contrast between this drawing room and Lord Clegg's, where Miss Featherstone's mother had grown up. In size, there was a great disparity. The Featherstones' was only a fourth as large as the one at Clegg House where he and his brother had called the day before. In quality of furnishings, though, the two dissimilar rooms were on equal footing.

Slade suspected the late Lady Mary must have furnished these rooms as a young bride. The mahogany furnishings were of very fine quality. While faded, the red and gold silken upholstery was still exceptionally lovely. No Italian masters adorned the walls here, but he recognized a Gainsborough. Was that Lady Mary? He could not say the lovely woman in the painting looked anything like Miss Featherstone, but as he peered at it he realized a strong resemblance between the woman in the flowing blue silk gown and towering powdered hair and Lady Sarah. They were obviously aunt and niece.

He wondered if Lady Mary ever regretted that she'd not wed a titled man with deep pockets. His mother had told him the Featherstones' marriage had been a true love match. He would have liked to have known the woman who was possessed of such great sense. For there was no finer man than Harold Featherstone.

How fortunate Lady Mary had been to be able to follow her heart.

If the late Lady Mary were anything like her daughter, she must have been possessed of uncommon intelligence. He could well understand how Harold Featherstone would have stood out from the other dandies who were sure to have been dancing attendance upon her. He hoped her niece shared that.

Then he would stand a chance.

The Featherstone servant, a middle-aged woman, announced dinner. Since Lady Sarah was the highest-ranking female, Mr. Featherstone led her into dinner. As the highest ranking male, Lord Slade led Miss Featherstone into the dining room.

"I have arranged that you shall be seated next to my cousin," Miss Featherstone whispered. "Pray, dazzle her with your wit."

Somehow, he thought a striking physical appearance would hold more sway with Lady Sarah than a man of wit. What a pity.

He was seated to the right of Lady Sarah. At the opposite end of the table, Miss Featherstone served as hostess. It appeared she had taken Poppinbotham, who sat at her right, under her wing.

After the soup was consumed in silence, Mr. Featherstone passed the pickled beets. "I thank you," Lord Slade said. "It is so very good of you to have us, and I must say this table has never held such lovely delights." His gaze settled on Lady Sarah.

Mr. Featherstone laughed. "You're anything but subtle, my lord. Is my niece not lovely? She reminds me so of my late wife."

"Then you must have been an exceedingly fortunate man to have wed such a beautiful woman. I trust that Gainsborough in the drawing room was of your Lady Mary?" Slade asked.

"Yes to both. I was most fortunate, and yes, that is her portrait."

Once their plates were filled and eating had actually commenced, Lady Sarah addressed him. "So you are mad for all things political."

"That's true. I fear that makes my conversation dull to those who don't share my interest."

"My cousin tells me you are anything but dull, my lord. She positively gushes over your intelligence."

"Your cousin is too kind."

Lady Sarah's glance flitted to Mr. Poppinbotham, and her lips thinned. "Indeed, she is."

That gentleman could be heard to say, "When I get in Parliament, I have not decided if it would be best to have my coachman bring me with the full four-horse carriage, or if I should just come in my tilbury." He glanced down the table at Slade. "Which do you do, my lord?"

The Buffoon had not yet been elected to the lower chamber when he was already comparing himself to a member of the upper chamber! "I daresay you will not be pleased with my response, Poppinbotham, for I am undoubtedly one of the most frugal men in all of Parliament. I let Slade House, took lodgings close to Westminster, and I walk to the House of Lords every day we are in session."

"But, my lord," Poppinbotham exclaimed, "it is dark when sessions end. Surely a fine aristocrat like yourself doesn't walk the pavement alone at night!"

"I am fortunate in that my colleagues are always gracious about giving me a lift at the end of the day. Often we're going to the same homes for dinner or routs."

"Or to your clubs, I daresay," Poppinbotham added.

"It's been a long while since I've been to Brook's." The fact was, it was too bloody expensive for Lord Slade to keep his membership active. Not when he still had three sisters to dower.

Mr. Featherstone obviously did not like the direction the dinner table conversation was taking for he began to steer it back to pertinent issues of the day. "Do you think, Lord Slade, the bill on labor unions will be put to a vote in the House of Lords?"

Slade shook his head. "Lord Carrington will never allow it to be brought up."

Mr. Featherstone's eyes narrowed with displeasure. "Might hit him in the pocketbook if he had to pay decent wages to the men who toil in his mines."

"Papa is an ally of Lord Carrington in this matter," said Lady Sarah, smiling broadly.

Her smile indicated she was inordinately pleased. Was the poor girl so ignorant of civil liberties that she was proud of her father's resistance to progressive reform?

Then it occurred to him she was merely pleased that she actually knew something about what they were discussing, that she had actually paid close enough attention to what was occurring in the chamber where her father served.

"My dear niece is well aware that her father and I do not see eye to eye on matters of reform, but we agree amiably to disagree," Mr. Featherstone said, smiling at Lady Sarah.

She peered across the table at Lord Slade. "I understand you have several sisters to launch into society, my lord."

"Three. The eldest will come out next year." It would take every farthing he could lay his hands on.

Unless he could capture an heiress.

He must make himself agreeable to Lady Sarah. More than that, he must make himself admire Lady Sarah. He had given his word to Miss Featherstone he would not ask for her cousin's hand until he could truthfully tell the lady he loved her. As it stood at present, the only thing he admired about the young lady was her appearance. And her hefty purse.

How had it been with his host when he had fallen in love with the previous Lord Clegg's daughter? "Tell me, Mr. Featherstone, prior to your marriage did your late wife share your interest in politics?"

"Indeed, she did. In fact, that is what brought us together." He glanced down the table at his daughter. "She was as astute as our daughter is. She used to sit in the galleries at the House of Commons – back when women were allowed – to watch her brother . . ." He turned to Lady Sarah. "That would have been your papa in the House of Commons before he succeeded. My dear Mary claimed she fell in love with me because she admired my speeches."

Slade nodded. "A most intelligent woman, to be sure."

At the other end of the table, he caught snatches about the extension of the franchise.

"You are in favor of giving the vote to the common man?" Poppinbotham asked Miss Featherstone.

"Of course, and you must, too, if you intend to align yourself with the Whigs."

"Oh dear." Lady Sarah wrinkled her nose. "Why, my dear cousin, should you wish to allow the masses to have a say in running our country?"

"It is my opinion that all men are created equal," Miss Featherstone replied.

"If it is permissible to disagree," Lady Sarah said, "I must. If our Creator had meant us to be equal, He would have made us equal. I believe it's we aristocrats who have been charged with looking after the masses."

"And some aristocrats do an admirable job," Lord Slade said, "but most are only interested in serving themselves."

Lady Sarah sighed. "Now I know why Papa does not attend these dinners." He turned to her. "I assure you, I do not mean to be disagreeable." But it was bloody difficult to be agreeable to one with whom he had nothing at all in common, to one whom he could not even admire.

After dinner, he contrived to be one of the last to leave in order to speak privately with Miss

Featherstone. Which meant he was privy to Poppinbotham's leave-taking from the young lady.

Holding her hand far too long, the Buffoon said, "I beg you allow me to call for you tomorrow afternoon for a ride in the park, my dear Miss Featherstone."

"If the weather obliges, that will be most agreeable, Mr. Poppinbotham."

Lord Slade was the last to leave.

"I am so happy to be alone with you, my lord," Miss Featherstone said, "for I must tell you to plan on Almack's Wednesday night."

He grimaced. He knew he must return there when his sisters were presented, but he had hoped to prolong the misery as long as possible. For there was nothing more boring than attending the assemblies there – where his title deemed him a matrimonial prize even without a fortune. The scheming mothers were relentless, the daughters were very young, and intelligent conversation was nonexistent. "Must I?"

She placed her hand on his sleeve. "If you hope to impress Lady Sarah with your elegance on the dance floor."

With no forethought of what he was doing, he placed his hand over hers. "I shall be greatly in your debt, my dear Miss Featherstone." Then he leaned toward her and dropped a kiss on her cheek before departing.

Chapter 7

Miss Featherstone was very pleased with herself. Despite that half the men in the *beau monde* had designs on her cousin, she had persuaded that lovely creature to ride to Almack's in Mr. Poppinbotham's carriage with her – and Lord Slade. Dear Sarah was sure to fall in love with the handsome earl after being so intimately in his company on these several occasions now.

On Wednesday night, they sped toward King Street with Miss Featherstone seated next to Mr. Poppinbotham in the dimly lit carriage. This afforded her the opportunity to observe the couple seated across from her. What a fine looking couple they made, Lord Slade so dark and handsome, Sarah so fair and lovely. In her soft ivory gown, draped elegantly over her smooth curves, Lady Sarah brought to mind an elegant Grecian goddess.

"You have the vouchers?" Mr. Poppinbotham asked Miss Featherstone, nervously.

She looked up at her companion. "Oh, yes, in my reticule. Should you like them?"

"What is the protocol?"

"I'm not sure there is a protocol. Do you know of one, Lord Slade?" Jane asked.

"Daresay it won't matter, but it may make Poppinbotham feel better if you allow him to present the vouchers."

Mr. Poppinbotham wiped his moist brow. "Oh, yes, very good of you, my lord, to suggest that."

Miss Featherstone handed over the vouchers.

"Any other protocols I should know about?" Mr. Poppinbotham asked.

"My mama says it's not proper to stand up with the same partner for more than two sets," Lady Sarah offered.

"Unless one is engaged to be married," Miss Featherstone added.

Mr. Poppinbotham nodded. "That is most helpful to know. Shouldn't wish to break any rules."

After arriving at the Palladian structure filled with hundreds of fashionably dressed members of the *ton,* the two couples immediately paired up to dance the first set, a minuet. When it was over, Lord and Lady Wycliff joined them.

"What the devil are you doing here tonight?" Lord Slade asked his friend. "I thought Almack's held the same appeal for you as reading *Ackermann's.*"

"Right you are, old boy, but when Louisa told me you'd be here tonight, I thought I'd come along. Never see you at White's or Brook's anymore."

"I'm honored."

"Don't be. I merely wanted to impart something to you." He moved to Lord Slade and settled an arm around his friend's shoulder, then he tilted his head back to the others. "Forgive me if I steal away Lord Slade." He affectionately eyed his wife. "I expect you, my love, will not lack for dancing partners whilst we are gone."

Indeed, hoards of young men swooped down to beg that Lady Wycliff and Lady Sarah stand up with them. Lady Sarah accepted Captain St. John's offer, and Louisa Wycliff went off with an older gentleman Jane did not know.

Jane and Mr. Poppinbotham then found chairs upon which to sit and watch the dancers.

* * *

The two lords who'd forged a lifelong friendship at Eton found a small chamber not being used. Though it lacked candles, a fire had been lain, so the room was not in total darkness. Wycliff closed the door.

"You act as if there's some sense of urgency," a baffled Slade said.

"There is. Darrington-Chuff is going to stand for Parliament at Blythstone."

"That is disappointing. You and I know he's an ass, but with his fortune and the connection with the Duke of Griffin, he's as good as elected."

"We cannot permit that to happen."

Slade's brows lowered. "Why?"

"Because he's not only a staunch Tory, he's dead set on strengthening the monarchy, emasculating Parliament, and opposing any kind of education for the masses."

Slade frowned. "I do remember him once saying that it was most dangerous to allow the common man to learn to read. *They were born to follow. We were born to lead.* Some kind of rot like that."

"Exactly."

"Then what do you propose we do about this?"

"We must persuade Alex to oppose him."

Slade considered the prospect for a moment. With assistance from his ducal brother, Alex Haversham might be able to absorb the hefty expense of electioneering, but it wasn't as if Alex had ever expressed an interest in political matters. Until very recently he'd been a soldier.

And there was also the fact he was a bachelor--not a serious-minded bachelor like Slade who was worn down with the cares of providing for younger siblings. Alex was a hard-drinking, fun-loving chaser of women. "We have no assurances Alex would bend to our ways. His brother, after all, is a Tory. And I doubt our dear friend would be interested in so serious a pursuit. He's living a rather hedonistic life at present."

"But back at Eton, it was decidedly apparent that our good friend's sympathies were firmly in the Whig camp."

"A lot has changed since we left Eton ten years ago."

"We must persuade him. You must. After all, it's said you're now the best orator in the House of Lords--and in the House of Commons before that."

Slade rolled his eyes. "Let us go see him tomorrow."

* * *

The three couples went to one of the supper rooms to procure lemonade and sit for a moment, though nearly every step of Lady Sarah's progress was impeded by the flocks of young men begging to stand up with her later.

Once they took their seats at one of the tables in the supper room, Lord Slade addressed the beauty. "This may be your only opportunity to sit down all night."

The lady took a tiny bite of her dry cake. "La, my lord! I am accustomed to it."

"I'm warning you, I mean to claim you for the last dance," he said.

"I should be honored."

Miss Featherstone was attempting to determine

if her cousin was truly interested in his lordship. It was difficult to tell by her actions because she was possessed of lovely manners. Even Mr. Poppinbotham, of whom Jane knew her cousin did not approve, was addressed by Lady Sarah in the most polite way imaginable.

Just that afternoon the cousins had discussed the prospective member of the House of Commons. "The man means to court you, Jane!" a shocked Lady Sarah had said.

"Indeed he does," Jane had replied.

"But, dearest, you are so far above that man's touch."

"But, dearest, he is *the* only man in three years who has ever honored me in such a manner."

"Well, I don't think you should encourage him. You know you can't marry him."

"Why can't I?" Miss Featherstone challenged, her brows lowered as she glared at her cousin.

"Because. Because you're much too fine for the likes of him. Surely you wouldn't even consider an offer from the man!"

Jane's stomach roiled when she answered. This was the first time she had ever acknowledged her tumultuous decision. "But I would."

Lady Sarah's jaw had dropped. "You cannot be serious! Can you honestly tell me you love the man?"

"I cannot tell you that."

"So you don't love him, but you'd be willing to marry him?"

"It's that or be dependent upon Robert and Lavinia once Papa . . ." She could not bear to put words to her thoughts.

"That's ridiculous! You can always have a home with me."

"That's very kind of you, but has it not occurred to you that I would one day like to have my own home? That I would like to become a mother and have a family of my own?"

The conversation had ended with Lady Sarah's eyes moistening over her cousin's plight.

When they finished their lemonade and dry cake in Almack's supper rooms, Lord and Lady Wycliff took their leave. "Call at Grosvenor Square tomorrow, Sinjin." Lord Wycliff said to Lord Slade.

Mr. Poppinbotham then begged Lady Sarah to stand up with him for the next set.

"And I should like to sit it out," said Lord Slade, eying Miss Featherstone. "Will you stay and amuse me?"

"Certainly, my lord." She glanced at her cousin, who was rising. "Neither Lord Slade nor I are especially fond of dancing."

After Mr. Poppinbotham and her cousin had left the chamber, Miss Featherstone addressed his lordship. "How do you think your suit is progressing with my cousin?"

"It's difficult to say. Lady Sarah is excessively agreeable to all of us who pay her court."

"Yes, I was thinking the same thing. A pity we can't contrive some disaster which would render you a great hero."

His black eyes glistened with amusement. "Like saving her from a swollen river, or rescuing her from a fire?"

"Exactly!"

"Pray, Miss Featherstone, I shouldn't want to be culpable in steering you on a path of deceit."

"Of course you wouldn't. You pride yourself on your exceeding honesty. Isn't that what got you into this situation in the first place? Your desire to fulfill a promise to your dying father?"

He grimaced, nodding.

"I do hope you are falling in love with my cousin. She has so many good qualities." *Other than her spectacular appearance and vast wealth.* "Indeed she does."

Not quite spoken like a man in love. The two needed more time together, Miss Featherstone decided. "I must change the topic of conversation, my lord, and beg that you assist poor Mr. Poppinbotham as he transitions from a mercantile world into our world. His political views cry out for guidance from someone like you, and I know he looks up to you."

So Miss Featherstone *was* aware of Poppinbotham's lack of attributes. "No one is better suited to guide the man than you."

"I thank you for the compliment."

"It wasn't meant for a compliment. It is the truth."

"You sound like my Papa."

"Your father is not only the most intelligent man of my acquaintance, but he is also clearly the most noble."

"I am in perfect agreement with you, my lord."

"A pity I'm not courting you. We are always in agreement, my dear Miss Featherstone."

Unaccountably, her stomach jostled. The very notion of his lordship courting her caused her heart to flutter, her breath to stutter. For she had been unable to shake from her thoughts the brotherly kiss he had dropped on her cheek a few nights earlier. While it may not have meant anything to him, it had meant everything to her. She had been profoundly moved over the kiss, even though it was not a *real* kiss.

The night of the kiss, with heart racing and thoughts morose, she had been unable to sleep.

Now, as she peered into his earnest face, she was compelled not to look away. Their eyes locked and her limbs began to tremble. Then her gaze flicked away. "It is a pity you're being forced into a courtship you would not have chosen, had you the luxury of free choice."

"Alas," he said, shrugging with resignation, "my bed is made, and now I must lie in it."

She straightened her gloves where they had wrinkled over her wrists, careful not to make eye contact with him. "Of course we both know you will be the most fortunate man in the three kingdoms if you can win my cousin's hand."

"Without question. There is no one better to meet all my needs than the lovely Lady Sarah."

She almost felt sorry for her beautiful cousin. Was Sarah's future as a wife intrinsically tied to her bounty, to her ability to meet her future husband's needs? What of love? There was, thankfully, the fact that Lord Slade had given his word. He would not ask for Lady Sarah's hand until he could truthfully tell Lady Sarah he loved her. Miss Featherstone had complete confidence in his lordship's honesty.

Lord Slade stood and offered her a hand. "Come, let us see how our former partners progress."

She froze for a moment as her eye traveled from the tip of his dark head, to his broad shoulders sheathed in fine black wool, to the starchy white cravat beneath his bronzed face. A well-tailored tail coat hugged his long torso. Her gaze then whisked over his long, powerful legs. How could silly Sarah not have fallen madly in love with such a magnificent man? Jane rose and placed her hand in his, not without a renewal of that fluttering in her heart.

When they reached the large assembly room, they backed up near the wall and surveyed the dancers. By now Mr. Poppinbotham and Lady Sarah had paired up with fresh partners. Miss Featherstone watched with amusement as her cousin danced with Lord Slade's brother, Captain St. John. The captain looked exceedingly handsome in his red regimental coat and white breeches which clung to his long, sinewy legs. It did not escape Miss Featherstone's notice that every unaccompanied miss in the chamber was watching the handsome young officer.

When the orchestra stopped playing, the others joined up with Jane and Lord Slade, and the brothers began to chat amiably.

Mr. Poppinbotham neared Miss Featherstone and lowered his voice. "You must point out which gentlemen here are Members of Parliament."

For the remainder of the evening, Mr. Poppinbotham, dressed in several shades of blue – except for his waistcoat which was of orange silk – escorted Miss Featherstone about the lofty chamber as she introduced him to men who had been elected to Parliament, most of them younger sons and younger brothers of peers.

No matter what part of the room she found herself in, Miss Featherstone felt Lord Slade's eyes on her. She supposed he was every bit as snobbish as Sarah in his views toward the unfortunate Mr. Poppinbotham and his connection with her.

She was just going to have to become inured to that.

* * *

On the ride home that night, it was all Slade could do not to try to stuff something into Mr. Poppinbotham's mouth to silence the pompous ass. And he just might if the man once more uttered, "When I get in Parliament. . ."

"The redhead in pink with whom I danced," Mr. Poppinbotham asked Miss Featherstone, "does she hail from a noble family, too?"

"Though she has no title like my cousin," Miss Featherstone nodded at Lady Sarah, "like me, she has connections. Her father is the third or fourth son, I can't remember which, of the Marquis of Hever. Can you enlighten Mr. Poppinbotham more than I?" Miss Featherstone directed her attention at the earl.

"Good heavens, no," Slade said. "I couldn't possibly keep up with how many sons Hever's sired or in what order they were born. I tip my hat to you, Miss Featherstone."

"Nor could I remember such insignificant information," Lady Sarah said. "Cousin Jane is blessed with an extraordinary memory."

"Indeed," Slade said.

"Miss Featherstone's intelligence has certainly been my observation," a self-satisfied Mr. Poppinbotham declared as he smiled at the lady being discussed. "She will make my entry into Parliament all the smoother, to be sure."

Lord Slade glared across the dark carriage. "Have a care not to put the cart before the horse, Poppinbotham."

"Certainly, your kind lordship. Electioneering comes before the prominence."

The man was exasperating. "May I hope your desire to enter Parliament is not to achieve prominence but to serve those who have elected you?"

"Of course, my lord. I am motivated by nothing save a burning desire to serve my fellow countrymen."

Not bad. A pity the lout was so insincere. If only the fellow had decided to stand for Blythstone instead of Plymouth. With his own hefty purse and guidance from Slade and Wycliff, along with the idealistic Miss Featherstone, he could have been a formidable threat against Darrington-Chuff.

Now it remained for Alex.

If only they could persuade him.

$\mathcal{C}$hapter 8

To Slade's surprise, Alex joined them the following morning as the three long-time friends assembled in the library of Wycliff's Grosvenor Square house. While Slade and Wycliff, both being dark-haired and taller than average, had always resembled one another, Alex looked vastly different. He was of average height and powerfully built. His hair had been quite blond when they were youths, but now it was a tawny brown, much like his skin had become after so many years on the Iberian Peninsula.

"I will own, Sinjin, I found Wycliff's message rather cryptic," Alex said as he looked up from his seated position on a leather chair near the fire where Wycliff stood. "And why in the devil did I have to be here so wretchedly early in the morning? It is not my custom to rise before afternoon."

Slade--still referred to as Sinjin by these two oldest friends--chuckled as he came to sit on a velvet settee facing the two. "Wycliff has an important matter he wishes to broach with you-- something that must be done in person."

Alex spun around to face his host. "What subject?" Given that he was the son of a duke, he was referred to as Lord Alex by everyone save these two life-long friends who only used the courtesy title in public.

"Your two best friends desire that you stand for Parliament." Wycliff peered at Slade.

Alex took a negative stance, holding up both palms. "Wait, wait! Has it never occurred to you that I have *no* interest in doing such a thing? Zero interest, to be precise."

"It's not only that the three of us always pledged to do everything together," Slade added, "but there's also the fact it's critical to everything we believe that you defeat Darrington-Chuff."

Alex's eyes widened. "Darrington-Chubb!" He used the name fellow Etonians had called their old foe. "He's the last man I'd expect to see in Parliament."

"Apparently he's decided governing holds more allure than race meetings at Newmarket," Wycliff said.

"Or shooting puppies for sport," Slade quipped.

Alex turned up his nose. "Never could tolerate the fellow."

Slade nodded. "With good reason."

"It's my belief he's set his sights on the House of Commons merely to thwart Sinjin and me at every turn. We represent the reforms he's determined to stop."

"He always was jealous of anything we did," Alex said.

"His jealousies were more than envy." Slade frowned. "They were sheer hatred."

"Yes," Alex said, "that's the Darrington-Chuff I remember. So what the devil does he promulgate?"

"If he had his way, he'd take us back four hundred years to the days of absolute monarchy and beheading those who disagree with said monarch," Wycliff said.

Alex nodded. "There would have to be something in it for him."

"All the man wants is to be in with those who possess power," Slade said. "Preferably with the king. An all-powerful king."

"Something like he always wanted at Eton. He wanted to be popular like we were." Alex shrugged. "Not that I'm boasting."

"You're not. You *were* the most popular lad at Eton, and your popularity extended to Sinjin and me because we were your closest friends," Wycliff said.

"That's just another reason why you're the most well qualified to defeat Darrington-Chuff."

"If it's public speaking that bothers you," Wycliff said, "you must know that Sinjin's become what many believe to be the greatest orator in the House in Lords. He can give you pointers when you stand for Blythstone. He learned a thing or two about electioneering when he served in the House of Commons before he succeeded."

"Who says I'm going to stand for Blythstone?" Alex's eyes narrowed with suspicion.

"We do." Slade poured a cup of coffee into an eggshell-thin porcelain cup which bore the Wycliff family crest. He went to hand it to Alex. "Coffee?"

"I need something stronger."

His friends ignored his comment.

Alex regarded them from beneath lowered brows. "I know you've always been passionate about politics, Sinjin, but Wycliff's purported interest has somewhat baffled me. Even though I was out of the country for a great many years, as was Wycliff, I was told that his first year back in England he had no interest in taking his seat in the House of Lords."

"You're right," Wycliff said. "My wife's the passionate one. She and her friend Miss Featherstone know more about what's happing in Parliament than half the members of the House of Lords."

"The two women are very intelligent." Slade looked at Wycliff. "Perhaps you can tell him about the Lewis chap. Alex would never betray a confidence."

Wycliff nodded and drew a deep breath. "My wife . . . is Philip Lewis. You've read him?"

"Everyone has! But what are you saying, man?" Alex asked.

"I'm saying that before we were married my lovely Louisa began writing her political essays under the name Philip Lewis."

Alex looked perplexed. "But he's brilliant."

"Not he. She," the other two men said at once.

"You must never tell another soul," Wycliff warned.

None of them spoke for a moment.

"The fact you must agree with Louisa's well-thought-out pleas for reform," Wycliff said, "speaks to the fact you would represent the same things Sinjin and I stand for."

"My head is spinning," Alex said, "and it's not from last night's brandy. Are you saying your new-found passion for reform was fed by your wife?"

Wycliff shook his head. "No. My wife merely awakened in me the same ideals you and Sinjin and I discussed at length when we were lads at Eton. Ideals that now need your voice."

Alex watched the waning fire and said nothing for several minutes. "Then everything Philip Lewis has ever written about--things like penal reform and compulsory education and extending the franchise--are things you two stand for in the House of Commons?"

"Yes," Wycliff answered. "And unless those years on the Peninsula have dramatically changed you, I believe those are things you also believe."

"I will own, such a voice is needed in the House of Commons, but you know I am not a good speaker," Alex said.

"Sinjin will help you."

"I'll also accompany you on every electioneering rally and will be happy to endorse you in the highest platitudes."

Alex groaned. "It would be bloody difficult to beat someone as wealthy as he is."

"Surely your brother would help," Wycliff suggested.

"But my brother's a Tory!"

Wycliff shrugged. "You needn't tell him at first what faction you align yourself with. I'm not asking that you lie. Just don't be altogether forthcoming about your principles."

Alex, his face so serious it looked stern, sat silently for several moments before he finally stood. "It truly grieves me to have to turn you down. I'm just not cut out for such serious pursuits. I do not desire to settle down. I do not desire a respectable marriage. I do not desire to sit in Parliament even if I do agree with the principles you stand for. I fancy spending my time in the enthusiastic pursuit of fine brandy and women of compromised morals."

$\mathcal{C}$hapter 9

Slade looked from the carriage window and saw that they were stopping in front of the familiar bow window of White's. "But I thought you were a member of Brook's," he said to Lord Wycliff.

"I am--because that's where the Whigs gather, but I also belong to White's because it was my father's club."

The coach door opened, and he stepped out.

"But why are you bringing me here tonight?" Slade asked.

"I hope for a confrontation with Darrington-Chuff."

"Good lord, why?"

As White's porter held open the door for the men to enter, Harry Wycliff paused. "Because he's been spreading lies about you and me."

Surely no one would believe Darrington-Chuff, who was noted for lying.

Wycliff purposely bumped elbows. "Look who's here."

Slade fully expected to look up and see Darrington-Chuff's corpulent body but instead saw Alex playing faro. A closer look confirmed that he was playing for low stakes. They went to greet him.

"When I finish here, I'll join you for a drink," Alex told them.

They settled at a table where they were

promptly served Wycliff's favored brandy, and a few minutes later Alex joined them. Though the room where they sat was subdued and quiet, the same could not be said for the next chamber. The volume of voices there must be in proportion to the volume of their liquor consumption.

Wycliff's brows lowered. "Does that not sound like Darrington-Chuff's voice?"

The faces of the other two men plunged into concentration. "So it is," Slade said. "Shall we see if he maligns us?"

They grew even more quiet as they listened.

"We Tories are still the majority, but we've got to stay that way. It's a good thing you're standing for Blythstone." Slade did not recognize the speaker's voice.

"Yes," Darrington-Chuff said. "I can no longer stand idly by whilst the likes of Wycliff and Slade try to destroy our nation. Who does that Wycliff think he is? Absenting himself for nearly a decade from the country he professes to love, then waltzing back here with ruinous plans? And where the devil did he find that wife of his? She's not one of us, though I don't mind saying I wouldn't mind sampling her fetching wares."

Wycliff, his face blanched with anger, leapt from his chair, stormed into the next room, and hurled his fist into Darrington-Chuff's fleshy cheek, sending that man backward. Darrington-Chuff slammed against a table, then, not able to right himself, slumped to the ground, blood gushing from his mouth.

Slade and Alex held Wycliff back. As angry as he was, he might kill the man sprawled on the flood beneath him.

Darrington-Chuff looked up at his attacker, a

cloudy expression on his face, fury firing his pale blue eyes. "You've knocked out my bloody teeth!"

"I'll do worse if you don't apologize for insulting my wife."

Silence greeted Wycliff's statement. Darrington-Chuff's blue eyes locked with Wycliff's brown. Not a sound could be heard as the two glared at each other. Darrington-Chuff finally bowed his head. "Meant no disrespect toward Lady Wycliff." Then eyeing one of his companions, he said, "Pray, Mulgrave, give me a hand up."

Once Darrington-Chuff was on his feet, Alex approached him. "Be warned, Darrington-Chuff, I shall defeat you for the Blythstone seat." With that, he turned, facing his friends. "Come, let's plan my victory, gentlemen."

The three longtime Eton friends left the chamber.

* * *

The following afternoon the three men once again met in Wycliff's library. Wycliff smiled at Alex. "I can't convey to you how happy I was to get your note."

"The note saying I refuse to meet with you before one in the afternoon?"

Slade laughed. "That--as well as the good news. We will be indebted to your brother for his generosity."

"I daresay Freddie thinks this will keep me out of mischief. The last time he came to my aid it was his brilliant idea to give my sweet little opera dancer an annuity to keep her from claiming my affections. Freddie fears I'll marry beneath my station." Alex shrugged. "Little does he realize that marriage has no appeal for me."

"I daresay he'll find having a brother in

Parliament distinguishes the family." Slade swigged his coffee.

"You must own," Wycliff said, "serving in that august chamber vastly eclipses being falling down drunk at Mrs. Nelson's gaming establishment."

Alex rolled his eyes. "Which, lamentably, I've been known to do."

"Now you shall become most distinguished," Wycliff said. "You'll start Saturday. There's to be a gathering of voters in Blythstone. Slade and I are coming with you, and we hope to show a force with other members of Parliament."

Alex gave a mock quiver. "I shall feel as if I'm parading about naked."

"It does rather feel that way the first time one speaks in public--especially when one is speaking about things that elicit an emotional response." Slade shook his head. "Whenever I address the topic of child laborers I have difficulty reeling in my emotions."

"Daresay it would be simpler to speak in superlatives about king and country," Alex said.

Wycliff nodded, disdain showing on his face. "Like the Tories."

Slade held up his palm. "Perhaps it's best whilst one is electioneering not to get too specific about reform. That can come *after* you're elected."

"I suspect that's good advice," Wycliff said.

"We don't need to give Darrington-Chuff ammunition with which to annihilate me."

"Our first order of business comes tomorrow night," Wycliff said. "I've begun asking prominent Whigs from both houses to gather here for the first of what I hope are political dinners. I propose to have these every week while Parliament's in session."

Alex rolled his eyes. "You two act as if you live and breathe nothing but Parliament. Slade doesn't even go to his club anymore."

"Lord Slade," said Lord Slade, "doesn't have the funds to belong to a club, nor can I afford to keep a town house."

"Exactly why I live in bachelor's lodgings," Alex said, then eyed Wycliff. "It's a good thing one of us has re . . . re*claimed* his family's fortune."

"And now our friend. . ." Slade eyed Wycliff, "has directed his abundance of energies on political reform."

"I had no choice. My dear wife is more passionate about politics than Slade and half the Whigs in Parliament."

"I confess I've had something to do with Wycliff's plan to begin having these political dinners. Mr. Featherstone has long been hosting smaller affairs for members of the House of Commons, and the last time I attended it became obvious to me that it's become a financial burden on him."

Wycliff laughed. "So my dear friend said, *Why not let Wycliff absorb the expense*?" He shrugged. "Which I'm most happy to do. Louisa's been wanting us to have these dinners since the day we wed."

"A most intelligent woman, to be sure," Slade said.

"Of course. She had the good sense to marry me."

* * *

Jane wrapped the rug around her against the night's chill and addressed her father. "It was very thoughtful of Lady Wycliff to send her coach to collect us." She felt guilty that poor Mr.

Poppinbotham was being excluded from the political dinner she was to attend that night at Wycliff House, but as she wasn't the host, she had no influence over the invitees.

"I've never even met Lord Wycliff," her father said. "Can't imagine why he desires my presence at the dinner."

"He wants you there because you're the leading Whig in the House of Commons."

"My dear daughter is prone to exaggerate my importance."

"As you exaggerate about me, Papa, when you say I'm pretty."

A frown pierced his aging face. "That is not an exaggeration. You *are* pretty. I can tell others think so, too. Mr. Poppinbotham as well as Lord Slade."

The mention of Lord Slade thinking her pretty sent her stomach plummeting. "You are mistaken about Lord Slade. Can you not tell he means to court my lovely cousin?"

"He may intend to court Lady Sarah, but I've seen the way he looks at you. I am not so aged that my eyesight is gone. Lord Slade admires you greatly."

"I will own, he does admire my mind."

"Harrumph!"

When they entered Wycliff House on Grosvenor Square, Lady Wycliff greeted them. After telling Mr. Featherstone how much she admired him, Lady Wycliff spoke to Jane. "Oh, Miss Featherstone, I am so happy you're joining us. I've been exceedingly eager for us to start hosting these affairs."

"Plural?" Jane asked.

"Yes, we hope to make them a weekly affair

while Parliament's in session."

"And members of the House of Commons will be asked as well?"

"Naturally."

Jane was relieved. If Lord and Lady Wycliff took over the hosting of these dinners, her father would no longer have to deplete their coffers. She thought of Mr. Poppinbotham and almost asked if candidates would be invited but realized it wasn't her place to bring up the subject. She was fortunate enough to be invited here tonight. It wasn't as if she had ever done anything to merit such consideration.

In the dining room where twenty of them sat down at a long, linen-covered table, Jane was mesmerized by the portrait that dominated the chamber. A Gainsborough of an uncommonly pretty woman. "Pray, Lady Wycliff, who is that beauty?" Her eyes lifted to the portrait.

Lord Wycliff proudly answered. "That is my mother."

"She's very beautiful," Jane said. Several more at the table concurred.

"Yes, she was," Lady Wycliff said. "Were it not for that portrait, I would not be sitting here as Harry's lady for we never would have married."

All eyes turned to their beautiful hostess. "After Harry's absence from England, he returned to this house to reclaim it, and the portrait was missing. It's a long, complicated story, but he enlisted my help to find it, and during our quest, we . . . fell in love."

Lord Wycliff looked proudly down the table to his wife. "So I like to say my mother helped me find the woman of my dreams."

How fortunate they were to have married for

love. A pity Jane would never be able to do so. She thought of Lord Slade. He, too, was prohibited from choosing a compatible mate.

Halfway through dinner that would have done credit to the Prince Regent, their host cleared his throat. "One of the reasons I've brought all of you together tonight--other than continuing to bond with like-minded reformers--is that I wish all of you to get to know Lord Alex Haversham, who has consented to challenge Hugh Darrington-Chuff for the Blythstone seat."

The young man being spoken of was seated beside Lord Wycliff and appeared the same age. She had noticed him as soon as she'd entered the house. It wasn't every day such a handsome man entered one's sphere. He wasn't classically handsome as was Lord Slade. Where Lord Slade was large and dark and somewhat brooding in appearance, Lord Alex displayed a sunny countenance with a ready smile that called attention to the piercing dimple in a single tanned cheek. Gold tones glistened in his fair brown hair.

Several men's voices lifted in approval.

"Is he not the son of the old Duke of Fordham?" Mr. Featherstone asked.

Lord Alex nodded.

From the quality of his well-tailored clothing, Jane could well believe he was the son of a duke.

"I was at Oxford with your father," Mr. Featherstone said. "I was very sorry to hear of his passing--and the passing of your eldest brother."

Lord Alex inclined his head and murmured his gratitude.

"There's to be an electioneering gathering in Blythstone Saturday," Lord Wycliff said, "and I have hopes many of us can come to show our support. Lord Slade means to speak, and Lord Alex will say a few words."

"Then I take it his brother, the Duke of Fordham, means to sponsor him," Lord Aylesbury said.

Alex nodded.

"But is your brother not aligned with the Tories?" Mr. Goldfinch asked.

"He is," Alex responded, "but he's typically apolitical, hence he's never been interested in taking his seat in the House of Lords."

"It's glad I am to hear that someone's got the funds to wage a campaign against Darrington-Chuff," Lord Babbington said. "Never cared for the fellow."

Lord Framptingham's brows lowered. "Did you say Blythstone? My wife has a fine little manor house near there. I propose all of us stay there Saturday. In support of Lord Alex, of course."

"That would be splendid," Lord Slade said.

"I must come," Louisa Wycliff said, eyeing her husband at the opposite end of the table.

"But, love, you'd be the only woman," her husband said.

Lady Wycliff looked at Jane. "Please, Miss Featherstone, say you'll come with me."

Jane could not believe her good fortune. Nothing could please her more than having the opportunity to spend a few days with these leading Whigs. "I should be happy to accompany you, my lady."

$\mathcal{C}$hapter 10

As she rode in the coach next to Lady Wycliff and directly across from that lady's husband and Lord Slade, Jane felt guilty for not inviting her cousin on this trip to Blythstone. She had given the matter a great deal of thought but decided that since Sarah had no interest in politics, exposing her to such a large dose of his lordship's passion would do nothing to strengthen any budding relationship between them. If anything, being around all these men who lived and breathed Whig politics would destroy any attraction Sarah might develop toward Lord Slade.

Jane felt guilty, too, for excluding Mr. Poppinbotham. She had asked Lord Slade if he thought Mr. Poppinbotham's own campaign could profit from attending the electioneering activities in Blythstone. "Pray, do not invite the man," Lord Slade had answered most emphatically. "Allow him to spend his efforts on his own electioneering."

Now, as they were nearing the end of their journey into Hertfordshire, she felt even more guilty. "Lord Slade, do you think Mr. Poppinbotham will expect us to join his electioneering efforts in Plymouth since we've done so for your friend Lord Alex?"

"Good Lord, I hope not. The man has to realize that Lord Wycliff's and my friendship with Lord

Alex goes back more than twenty years. The three of us are like brothers. We'd go to the ends of the earth for one another."

"In fact, Alex and you *have* gone to Land's End for me," Lord Wycliff said to his friend, grinning. Then he directed his attention to Jane. "I daresay Poppinbotham will never be able to make such a claim on us."

"And," Lady Wycliff added in a kindly voice, "Plymouth *is* much farther than Hampshire. I'm sure Mr. Poppinbotham will never expect you to travel that far."

"If the three of you men are such great friends, how is it that I'd not heard of Lord Alex before?" Jane asked.

The two men looked at each other sheepishly. Finally, Wycliff shrugged. "Lord Alex has heretofore had other matters to occupy him."

"Yes, he spent several years as a soldier, only returning just this last year," Lord Slade said.

Jane's thoughts returned to Mr. Poppinbotham. She knew Lord Slade was in the same camp as her cousin in disliking an alliance between herself and the printer, but at least Lord Slade had never come out and declared his opposition. He merely expressed it in his facial expressions and tone of voice when speaking about Jane's suitor. Her first-ever suitor.

She'd been flattered over Mr. Poppinbotham's disappointment in learning that she was going to be gone for several days--even though he lacked any of the attributes Lord Slade held in abundance, Mr. Poppinbotham had most certainly endeared himself to her.

I must not look upon Lord Slade's perfection of person, she told herself. Consequently, she'd spent most of the journey either talking to Louisa Wycliff or eyeing Lord Wycliff's boots.

When they arrived at Lady Framptingham's manor house, Jane marveled that the Framptinghams did not even use this fine house. Both his lordship and his wife had inherited many properties throughout England and Scotland.

The house--Jane had since learned was called Stourside Manor--was constructed of Portland stone in the Palladian style, without wings. It was a single, three story block with a pedimented roof supported by Ionic columns and was set in a verdant parkland that terminated in a circular drive in front of the house's modest portico.

Once they entered the house, Lord and Lady Framptingham greeted them enthusiastically. At first Jane was a bit taken aback. Since Lord Framptingham was fairly young and of relatively handsome appearance, she had expected his wife to be of similar circumstances. Lady Framptingham, however, was at least ten years her husband's senior and was in no way attractive. She had grown to fat, and a thick roll of fat clung to her sunken chin. Jane could not help but to think Lord Framptingham had most likely *not* married for love. Apparently, his wife was a great heiress.

The lady proved friendly and gracious to her guests, and Jane instantly admired her.

Lord Alex had reached Stourside before them. "The things I do for my friends," he lamented to Lord Slade, his voice low, but not so low that Jane could not hear him. "To think I could have been with Mrs. Thaxton, the toast of the London stage tonight, yet, here I am, preparing for dull electioneering just to join Wycliff and Sinjin."

"We did vow before we ever left Eton to help one another," Lord Slade reminded him, "and we desperately need you now."

Lord Alex's brows lowered. "Because of that vile Darrington-Chuff."

As they climbed the broad stone staircase, Lord Wycliff nodded. "I'm afraid so. The man has continued to spread lies about our agenda. He's telling the Tories that we're plotting a people's revolution like what the French experienced two decades ago."

"Does he not realize that we *are* aristocrats? Why would we want to sever our own heads?" Lord Slade asked.

Lord Wycliff shrugged. "His brain never was more developed than that of a newborn colt's."

"Then why in the devil do the Tories tolerate him?" Lord Framptingham asked.

Lord Slade shrugged. "He *is* very wealthy, and his great uncle *is* a duke."

"I've sent my secretary to spy at Darrington-Chuff's electioneering meeting today," Lord Framptingham announced.

A wicked smile swiped across Lord Slade's face. "Excellent!"

The Framptingham servants showed the newest arrivals to their chambers, where they would stay until dinner.

Jane was pleased over her apple green bedchamber. Its ceilings were tall, its proportions generous, and though the silken draperies and bedcoverings were faded, she thought the room lovely. She always marveled at how the very wealthy owned such lavish houses that were seldom used.

As she changed from her traveling clothing to

dress for dinner, it occurred to her that she was surely the only lady here without a personal maid. Of course, there were only three ladies at Stourside.

* * *

A dozen of them had sat down to dinner around the Framptinghams' generous table. In addition to the four who'd come in Wycliff's carriage and their hosts and Alex, five solo Whig members of the House of Lords had come. The food--from fresh fish to kidney pies and roast saddle of lamb along with a wide assortment of side dishes--far surpassed the tolerable fare Slade had expected from a little-used country house staff.

The conversation was exactly the stuff on which Slade thrived. Every man--and woman--at the table held views which paralleled his own.

The congeniality of the night, however, halted as if shot by an arrow when Framptingham's secretary, his brows lowered, entered the dinner room to report on what had transpired at Darrington-Chuff's electioneering.

Framptingham asked his man, a Mr. Howard, to pull up a chair next to him. "Now, pray, Mr. Howard, tell us what has agitated you so."

The secretary drew a deep breath. "The gathering was very well attended. Even the candidate's great uncle, the duke, came, and his presence had the assemblage in awe of sharing a humble chamber with such a personage."

Slade observed the forty-year-old secretary with respect. This wasn't the first time he'd had dealings with him. Not only was Howard well spoken, but he was also possessed of a fine mind.

"But the worst of it was," Mr. Howard continued, "that Mr. Darrington-Chuff--and his great uncle--told monstrous lies about you, my lord. You and Lord Alex Haversham."

Lord Framptingham's eyes narrowed. "What kind of lies?"

"He used the word *anarchists* to describe you, but it's my belief he's not acquainted with the proper meaning of the word. I believe he meant to label you and the other prominent Whigs as *revolutionaries*."

"Either way," Slade said with disgust, "it's an outrageous lie."

A moment later, Alex tried to adopt a flippant air. "I say, did the imbecile say anything else derogatory about me?"

"That," Lord Framptingham said to his secretary, "is Lord Alex Haversham."

Mr. Howard peered across the table at Alex. "Indeed he did, my lord. He said until you took the whim to stand for Parliament, you had led a life of complete debauchery."

Wycliff shook his head angrily. "That is the pot calling the kettle black."

Mr. Howard's comments struck anger in Slade's breast, but Alex appeared to handle such comments with nonchalance. He gave a bitter laugh. "Damned difficult to exhibit debauchery when one has spent eight years leading men into battle."

"The fool Darrington-Chuff is epically misinformed," said Wycliff, a grave expression on his face.

But how did one fight against such slanders, Slade wondered. He pushed away his plate. He'd lost his appetite. These lies sickened him. How could they counter these lies with the truth? Would anyone even come to Alex's gathering

Saturday? Had they come all this way for nothing? Did Alex not have a prayer of winning? Worst of all, would that baboon Darrington-Chuff beat a fine man like Alex, who would do good for his fellow man?

"How many would you say attended?" Wycliff asked.

"I counted chairs for around four hundred and fifty, and at least another hundred stood around the perimeter of the assembly hall."

"Did Mr. Darrington-Chuff serve food and drink to those who'd come to hear him speak?" Lady Framptingham asked.

"Only drink."

"Well," that lady said, a smile flitting across her full face, "I propose we show Lord Alex's supporters some aristocratic hospitality."

Her husband's eyes twinkled. "And what are you proposing, my lady?"

"We shall host a fete such as the residents of Blythstone have never seen, and we shall have it right here at Stourside Manor."

"But there's no way we can accommodate hundreds of people within the walls of this house!" her husband protested.

"We'll have tables spread over the grounds, and all attendees will have the opportunity to stroll through the manor's public rooms," Lady Framptingham responded.

Those seated went silent. Miss Featherstone was the first to speak. "You are exceedingly generous, Lady Framptingham. My papa, who's been in Parliament for more than forty years, swears that the best way to the voters' hearts is through their stomachs. And I might add that inviting the voters into an fine aristocratic manor house like this will not only be an incredible experience for them, but it will also solidify strong support for Lord Alex."

Now that she was not being held up for comparison with her physically flawless cousin, Slade thought Miss Featherstone looked quite pretty tonight. Though she was close in age to Wycliff's lovely lady, Jane Featherstone looked much younger. Perhaps it was the sprinkle of freckles across her nose, or perhaps it was the virginal simplicity of her ivory frock, but she did not look as if she could have left the school room. He rather admired the way the candlelight played off her cork-coloured locks. They no longer looked so plain at all.

She no longer looked plain.

And there was nothing even close to average about her intelligence. As always, he completely agreed with every word she said.

Lord Framptingham nodded pleasantly at Miss Featherstone, and then directed his attentions at his wife. "Well, woman, we'd better get started. You've got two days to prepare a feast the likes of which those men will never forget."

Lady Framptingham looked complacent. "When have I ever failed to pull off a respectable fete, my love?"

From his seat at the head of the table to his wife at the foot, Lord Framptingham beamed with pride. "Never, my dear. I am a most fortunate man to have wed you."

Slade looked from lord to his lady. Slade and most of those in the *ton* had always thought Framptingham had married for fortune, but now it was obvious that if Framptingham had not been in love with his wife at their marriage, he most certainly was in love with her now.

More than anything, Slade was impressed with the way Lady Framptingham's interests dovetailed with those of her husband. She was his helpmate in every way.

Try as he might, Slade could not picture Lady Sarah as his political helpmate. Even if by some unfathomable good fortune, that lady would respond favorably to his suit, he knew she would never share in his passion for governing.

He wondered if he would ever be able to fall in love with her. Certainly, she was extremely pretty, but he'd yet to be snared by Cupid's arrow. And he had promised her cousin he would not propose until he could truthfully declare his love for the beautiful heiress.

Damn, he should be in London this very moment dancing attendance upon her. He had an obligation to his family. He inwardly sighed. He also had an obligation to the people of England. Alex in Parliament could be just what this country needed.

What a pity that Alex's candidacy appeared now to be such an uphill battle.

"Say, Lord Alex," their host said, "could your brother, the duke, be persuaded to come here Saturday?"

Alex's face brightened. "As it happens, he's in London, which is a great deal closer than our family seat in Yorkshire. If we could dispatch a courier tonight, it's possible he could make it here by Saturday--though I cannot make any promises."

Lord Framptingham turned to a footman and asked that someone named Smith be fetched to travel to London that night.

"My papa, who was *not* in Parliament," Lady Framptingham said, "was always vastly impressed by those with titles--especially dukes. That's the way it is with those of us not born to the peerage." She smiled down the length of the table at her husband.

* * *

Jane had great admiration for Lady Framptingham. By the time Jane had awakened the following morning, the house was alive with workmen. Lady Framptingham and her hefty purse had succeeded in enlisting the services of a dozen more scullery workers and another two dozen footman, who were already busy setting up tables and chairs in the lovely parkland surrounding Stourside.

The lady of the house lamented that she did not have enough livery for the additional footmen, but that did not stop her from rummaging the attics for discarded livery from the past three generations.

"The important thing," Louisa Wycliff told Jane, "is that there are enough servants to serve the food. I daresay the attendees won't pay attention to what the footmen look like or what they're wearing."

Lady Framptingham hung up a musty coat in the scarlet livery on drying racks in her own bedchamber. "I daresay you're right."

The local greengrocer's supply had been depleted, and several local farmers fattened their purses by offering up their barnyard occupants for Lady Framptingham's fete for Lord Alex Haversham.

While all the activity was being conducted under the watchful eye of Lady Framptingham's capable housekeeper, Lady Framptingham, along with Lady Wycliff and Jane--all dressed as stylish as possible--piled into the plush Framptingham coach and began to pay calls on the gentry within eight miles of Stourside Manor.

"My mother, a Carter, was raised at Stourside Manor," Lady Framptingham told Louisa and Jane, "and our family has been one of the leading landowners in this part of the county for more than two hundred years. I still believe we can carry some weight hereabouts."

"I do hope you're right," Lady Wycliff said.

Louisa Wycliff and Jane had both been melancholy since dinner the night before. How did one wage a war against lies? Equally as upsetting, what kind of a Parliamentarian would Mr. Darrington-Chuff make when he didn't even know precisely what anarchy was?

If women were permitted to vote, Lord Alex would handily win on the basis of Lady Framptingham's easy intercourse with Stourside's neighbors, each of whom she knew by name. She would whisk in and reacquaint herself with the wife and ask to speak to the husband, and then she would launch into her invitation.

"Mr. Mather," she said to the solicitor on the outskirts of the village of Blythstone, "Lady Wycliff and Miss Featherstone have joined me in coming to invite you to a fete at Stourside Manor at two tomorrow afternoon for Lord Alex Haversham's candidacy for the House of Commons for Blythstone. We expect Lord Alex's brother, the Duke of Fordham, to attend as well and would be delighted to have you come and meet them." She eyed Jane. "You may have read about Miss Featherstone's father. Harold Featherstone has been in the House of Commons for forty years."

"Indeed I have heard of him." He smiled at Jane, then beamed back at Lady Framptingham. "I will be delighted to attend."

"I beg, Mr. Mather, that you bring any other voters you should know," her ladyship said.

"I would be honored, my lady."

* * *

At two o'clock Saturday Slade joined the men in the library. They had not closed the library door so they could hear when the prospective voters arrived. For once, Alex did not look calm. It wasn't just his nervousness over offering himself up to several hundred strange men, but Alex knew he was worried that his brother had not arrived.

"I feel beastly that Fordham's not come. I shouldn't like the voters to think we've lied about him attending," Alex said, his brows pinching together.

Lord Framptingham peered at the footed clock upon the mantelpiece. "What worries me is that it's two, and not a soul has come."

Chapter 11

The Duke of Fordham, Alex's brother, turned out to be the first to arrive. Alex enthusiastically introduced him to all the Parliamentarians who had gathered to support him, then Slade and Alex led him to the drawing room to introduce him to their hostess and the two other ladies.

"Her father is Harold Featherstone," Alex said after introducing Jane.

The duke's brows lowered. "The Whig?"

"Yes, your grace," she answered.

The duke's lips thinned, and then he politely took his leave of the women. "I beg a word with you, Alex."

The frigid tone of Fordham's voice made Slade uneasy. He watched as the brothers went into the morning room and closed the door.

When the two men reentered the library moments later, Alex's face was grim. The abrupt change in their manners went unnoticed by most of the men present because the corridors of Stourside began filling with men's voices as the first wave of visitors arrived.

"I'd best go greet them," Lord Framptingham said.

Slade approached Alex and spoke to him in a low voice. "Pray, what is the matter?"

Alex eyed the open doorway. "Come with me."

Slade followed his friend to a small china closet

off the dinner room. The chamber was ringed by white, glass-fronted cases displaying turquoise porcelain in every shape and size imaginable. This was the only room in the bustling downstairs where privacy could be obtained since the visitors had begun flocking to the manor house.

Alex's face was still sorrowful. "I shall be obliged to drop out of the contest."

Slade felt as if he'd been punched in the gut. "What's happened?"

"My brother refuses to support a Whig."

It was a moment before Slade could gather enough composure to respond. "I suppose we should have been honest up front." Slade had felt uneasy that Alex had evaded the most important topic when seeking assistance from his brother. "Though I will own, I thought he'd be more accepting."

"You're right, of course. I wish now I'd been more passionate in expressing my opinions. Who knows, I may have been able to convert him to our views. But it's too late now."

Slade nodded. "I believe we will have to accept that Fordham's not going to be able to help." He held up a palm. "That's not to say you need to give up today. We are expecting hundreds of guests-- guests who've come to see you. This is your opportunity to court them. Tomorrow we'll address the funding problem."

"I don't know how I can go out and be congenial the way I feel at present. It's as if Freddie's yanked the rug out from beneath my feet."

"Forget you're a person. Think of yourself as a vessel of change. You're not representing one man. You're representing thousands."

Alex drew a deep breath. "I don't see how this

can work."

"Somehow, it will." Slade found himself wondering how rich Wycliff was. Would he be able to bestow enough money on his friend to establish the campaign? But underlining everything was Slade's fear that they would not be able to raise the money, and Alex would have to drop out.

Today, though, they would plunge into electioneering with every intention of courting these voters. Today they would act as if victory were in their hands.

Knowing what a novice Alex was, Slade would have to stay close to his friend as he mingled with the guests. The two left the closet to face a stream of ruddy-faced men.

Slade's first instinct was to start introducing the candidate to his potential constituents, but these men were much too interested in the massive chambers and fine furnishings of Stourside. "Will you take a look at that chandelier over the staircase," said a middle-aged man who was clutching in his hand the hat he had recently removed from his ginger head.

It was best Slade and Alex wait until the men had finished gawking at the manor house that had been closed to them for decades.

Lord and Lady Framptingham, who had snagged the Duke of Fordham to stand beside them, stood in the drawing room greeting the men as they poured into the chamber. "Ah," Lady Framptingham said in a much louder voice, "Here is Lord Alex. I must introduce you to the man who's going to be the next great Parliamentarian to represent the good people of Blythstone."

Slade's normally gregarious friend had never appeared so reticent as he went to stand beside his stone-faced brother. Slade went to stand on his other side. "Smile," he instructed in a whisper. "And tell your bloody brother to be pleasant."

Surprisingly, Alex did as Slade told him.

As the line of men moved along, Slade shook their hands and introduced himself, careful to explain that he had been in Parliament since he was one-and-twenty.

"You look mighty young still," a gray-haired man told him.

"I shall be thirty on my next birthday," Slade answered. "I am the same age as Lord Alex, who was at Eton with me."

"So he's the son of a duke?" The next man said.

"Indeed."

Lady Framptingham moved to sandwich herself between him and his friend. Which was a good thing, given her family's association with these voters.

"Once we've had the opportunity to meet with all of you," she said "we're going outside where the tables have been set up to accommodate all of us for a feast. We're so happy you're able to join us."

* * *

Lord and Lady Wycliff, Jane, Lord Slade, Lord Alex, and his brother ate at the table with their hosts. Lord Slade came to sit next to Jane, who was seated at the opposite end of the table from her friend Lady Wycliff. Something was disturbing him. "Have things not turned out to your satisfaction, my lord?" she asked.

"Actually, I've been pleased both by the turnout and by Lord Alex's ability to speak intelligently with the voters."

"But something's wrong."

"You know me too well." He sighed. "Fordham

refuses to support his brother."

"It's my fault," she said, her stomach sinking. "I could see it in his face when the duke asked me who my father was. I'm usually proud to tell people I'm the daughter of Harold Featherstone, but I almost hated to do so in front of the stuffy duke. He's very unlike his brother."

"Yes, he is," Lord Slade said, grimly. "Don't blame yourself. The duke was bound to learn Alex sympathizes with the Whigs. It's best he learn as quickly as possible."

"But what will Lord Alex do?"

"I wish I knew."

"The Framptinghams are very wealthy."

Lord Slade frowned. "But Framptingham already sponsors a half a dozen seats. I'd hate to push them. The richer one is, the more financial obligations one has. Look at how much they have already done today for Alex."

"There is that."

"A pity I have nothing to contribute."

"As an impoverished Featherstone, I do understand that," she said with a nervous laugh.

"We have that in common, too." He offered her a wan smile.

"Lord Wycliff seems quite wealthy."

"I don't know how wealthy he is. When we first floated the subject of Alex standing for the House of Commons, Wycliff was the first to suggest he get the money from his brother."

"Oh dear. That's not good."

"No, but I still plan to ask him if he can assist Alex."

"What about Lord Alex? He is a duke's son. Does he not have money of his own?"

"There were three sons of the old duke--along

with four daughters to dower. Since Alex was the third son, there wasn't a lot for him."

"So he's just third in line to the dukedom?"

"Actually, the eldest son died last year shortly after ascending to the dukedom. He was just thirty when he died of a strangulated hernia after a game of tennis"

"I wonder if Mr. Poppinbotham would be able to help. He seems quite wealthy."

"No."

There was something akin to vehemence in Lord Slade's voice. She did wish others would be more tolerant of the man she might marry.

While they talked, she noticed that Lord Alex had not touched his food, but had finished his bumper of Madeira and had poured another glass from one of the decanters that dotted the table. Then, still clutching his bumper, he rose.

Lord Slade also rose. "It looks like he's going to mingle with the guests. I'd best accompany him."

She placed a hand on Lord Slade's arm. "Perhaps he needs to do this on his own. He mustn't look like another man's puppet."

Lord Slade sat back down. "You're right. As always."

She shook her head. "Would that your words were true!"

His lordship continued to watch his old friend as he moved amongst the long tables of men who had gathered there. "He's looking more like his old self. Alex was always our leader, always the merrymaker, always the lady charmer."

She could well believe that Lord Slade had never been the lady charmer. The very notion of him having a lady bird, as did other men born to rank and privilege, was as preposterous as Miss

Plain Jane Featherstone being a light skirt.

She peered down the table. The duke was chatting amiably with their hostess. Lady Framptingham did possess the ability to put others at ease. Now that their food was eaten, the Wycliffs moved down to speak with Jane and Slade.

"Why so grave?" Lord Wycliff asked as he pulled up a chair across the table from them. "I would say the event's been a spectacular success, and Alex is well on his way to charming every man here with his cheerful nature."

Lord Slade kept his voice low. "Fordham refuses to support his candidacy."

An angry look shot across Lord Wycliff's face. "Why in the devil not?"

"Because Alex is a Whig," Lord Slade said.

Lord Wycliff uttered a curse which Jane pretended not to hear. "Is there nothing we can do to persuade the man?"

"Had we time, possibly," Lord Slade answered. "As it is, there's not enough time."

"If only this weren't so late in the quarter," Lord Wycliff said. "I've drained my coffers sponsoring my cousin Edward Coke, who's married to Louisa's sister. He's electioneering in East Anglia. That--along with buying back the Grosvenor Square house--have left me with pockets to let until things come right next year."

"That's bloody bad news," Lord Slade said.

Jane felt as if she'd been struck. Deep down, she'd been confident that Lord Wycliff would come to his old friend's rescue. It never occurred to her Lord Wycliff was not fabulously wealthy. His lovely home, his wife's beautiful clothing, their fine carriage had all seemed to point to an inexhaustible source of income.

Lord Slade's gaze lifted toward the circular drive in front of the house. "Good Lord! You won't believe who's just arrived." There was uncharacteristic malice in his voice.

They all turned to look.

"He wouldn't. . ." Lord Wycliff said.

"Who wouldn't, darling?" his wife asked.

"Hugh Darrington-Chuff."

Now that she had a name, Jane realized the bloated man storming toward them had to be Darrington-Chuff. The arrogance of his stride was matched by the anger which clenched his fists and distorted his ruddy face.

Lord Slade leapt to his feet and moved to Lord Alex. The two then moved to intercept their opponent, who had almost reached the head table.

Anger simmered in Darrington-Chuff's pale eyes when he spoke to Lord Alex with a hatred so intense it made his voice tremble. "I. Will. Crush. You. You haven't a prayer against my fortune. I'd advise you to quit now and save yourself humiliation."

The two enemies' eyes locked.

"You cannot intimidate me, Darrington-*Chubbs*."

Lord Alex must be using a name the lads at Eton had called the portly Darrington-Chuff, Jane mused.

Hatred distorted the man's face as he lunged toward Lord Alex.

Two very large footmen intervened and held the intruder's arms behind him.

"I will buy the votes of half these men here," Darrington-Chuff threatened. "That's why I've come today."

Lord Framptingham stood. "No, you will not. Not on my property. Get. Out." With just a few nods to his other footmen, a half a dozen men closed around Darrington-Chuff and began to escort him from the property--but not quietly.

"Do not vote for Lord Alex Haversham," he shouted. "He wants to destroy our country! Do not trust him."

Jane could not help but to wonder how much damage had been done to Lord Alex's campaign. First, the loss of financial support, and now a slur against Lord Alex's good name.

"Just ignore him," Lord Slade said to his friend. "Come, let's show these voters what a bloody good fellow you are."

"Yes, I'd like to vouch for his character also," Lord Wycliff said.

The three of them began to move from table to table, shaking men's hands and speaking in a friendly manner.

What a contrast those three fine men were to the vile Mr. Darrington-Chuff, Jane thought. If only Lord Alex could procure the funds to buy these men's votes. She did not approve of the British electoral method. How she wished they would copy the Americans, who mandated secret balloting where voters voted for the best candidate--not the one who paid for their allegiance. She would have to speak to her friend, the essayist who secretly wrote as Philip Lewis. That would be a good topic for her next essay.

* * *

The Duke of Fordham brought out Jane's baser instincts. As she watched him take leave of the brother he'd so vastly disappointed, she resisted the urge to tear into him like a shrew. How could one brother betray another? It wasn't as if Fordham had ever committed himself to Tory principles before. The only other person to ever have incited in Jane such feelings of anger was her sister-in-law Lavinia. And now, too, Hugh Darrington-Chuff.

"Forgive me for withdrawing my support," Fordham said to Lord Alex.

"One day you'll see the error of your ways. One day you'll understand the reasons for my supposed defection," Lord Alex said. "I'm committed to what my Whig friends stand for. One way or the other, I will raise the money."

Once Fordham had driven off, Lord Alex explained to their host and hostess that his Whig affiliation had lost his brother's backing.

Lord Framptingham shook his head woefully. "That's a very low blow, indeed. Would that I could help, but I am already sponsoring a half a dozen other seats."

"You've already been exceedingly generous." Lord Alex turned to Lady Framptingham. "I am deeply indebted to you for all you've done."

"I wish I could do more," that lady said. "As it is, I can scrape together only three hundred to help your campaign. I believe in you."

Lord Wycliff nodded ruefully. "The most I can get my hands on before the next quarter is two hundred."

Lord Alex bowed his head. "I'm deeply appreciative. Those contributions, while not enough, will go a great way toward what I will need."

How Jane wished she had something to contribute. But she did have an idea.

Lady Framptingham came and linked her arm to Lord Alex's. "Come. You must tell me about all your conversations with the good people of Blythstone. You impressed them."

Lord Slade turned to Jane. "Can I persuade you to walk about the park with me?"

"Indeed you can." She linked her arm to his, and they went outdoors where it was a cool but sunny afternoon. "How fortunate we were to avoid rain today. I thought the feast went splendidly-- except for the wretched business with the wretched Duke of Fordham."

Lord Slade frowned. "That was unfortunate. Unpardonable, actually."

"I thought so too. Poor Lord Alex. I don't know how he managed to be so civil to his traitorous brother."

"My, I did not know Miss Jane Featherstone ever felt malice toward anyone," Lord Slade said with a chuckle. "Though, I will own, Fordham most certainly deserves your wrath."

"He most certainly has earned it. I don't know how one's brother could be so callous."

"I believe part of Fordham's problem is that he's always been jealous of Alex, who was a great favorite with their parents--as well as with anyone who's ever known him."

"Yes, I can see that. He's charming whilst being sincere. I was taken aback when he addressed Mr. Darrington-Chuff so offensively."

Lord Slade nodded. "Quite truthfully, though everyone at Eton addressed the blow-hard as Darrington-*Chubb*, I can honestly say that Lord Alex never did. One who's well liked never has a need to belittle one who's less fortunate. The only reason Alex did so today was because Darrington-

Chubb was behaving so beastly to him. Were it up to Alex, this would be a gentleman's race."

"But Darrington-Chuff is no gentleman."

"Precisely."

She could never tire of gazing upon Lord Slade's handsome profile, never tire of strolling beside him. Being next to his big frame made her feel undeniably feminine.

He drew a deep breath. "I cannot speak to you about your cousin in front of the others, so I thought now would be a good time. I had half hoped you'd have been able to persuade her to come on this journey with us."

The mention of her cousin was like being stabbed with her darning needle. "I gave the matter serious consideration, but in the end I thought being at a political gathering might do you more harm than good."

He quirked a brow.

"Surely you've noticed that Lady Sarah has no interest in political matters?"

He thought for a moment before answering. "I don't suppose I had. When one's life is consumed with one subject, one assumes everyone shares that passion, but now I see that you are right."

"It's a pity you may have to marry a woman with whom you have so little in common." As soon as she spoke, Jane wished she could take back her words.

"Yes," he said solemnly.

Her heart went out to him. What sacrifices he was prepared to make in order to fulfill his Vow. "Of course, I know you won't marry my cousin unless she completely owns your heart, and there is much to claim your love in Lady Sarah."

"Indeed."

She wanted to ask him if he were falling in love with her cousin, but she could not bring herself to do so. She had no right to probe into so personal a matter. And as supportive as Jane was to his pursuit, it still hurt her to think of him loving Lady Sarah. She sighed. Lady Sarah, for reasons Jane would never be able to understand, could never love Lord Slade as Jane was capable of doing. Not that Jane would allow herself to fully commit to loving this incredibly appealing man who towered over her at present.

He cleared his throat. "I don't suppose Lady Sarah has mentioned me?"

She shrugged. "At this point, my cousin has not been able to narrow down the considerably long list of her admirers."

"I wish I were a more patient man."

"Then you might have to make a rash decision you might live to regret. Let the affections grown naturally."

He placed a gentle hand over Jane's. "You are right. Once more."

* * *

After their walk, all of them gathered in the drawing room where Lord Alex announced that his brother had withdrawn his support. "My earnest commitment to court today's voters was in no way a commitment to this candidacy. I felt it my duty to be gracious to men who had given up their time to meet me, but I will not be able to proceed with electioneering without considerable financial support which has not been forthcoming."

Lord Wycliff came to stand beside Lord Alex. "I am happy to say that Lady Framptingham has pledge three hundred guineas to Lord Alex's campaign, and I've managed two hundred. Are any of the rest of you able to contribute?" He gazed from one to the other of the four peers who had come to Blythstone. The first shook his head ruefully. The second, Lord Babbington said, "One hundred is the most I can get my hands on. Bloody bad timing."

"I know," Lord Wycliff said. It's eight weeks until the next quarter."

"A pity the voters must be bribed *before* casting their votes," Lord Aylesbury said. "If only the election were to be held during the next quarter I would be able to make a sizeable contribution, but now, there is no way I can get my hands on another farthing."

When Lord Wycliff eyed the final peer, he slowly shook his head, a solemn look on his face.

Jane was more committed than ever to proceed with her plan.

$\mathcal{C}$hapter 12

On Jane's first day back in London, Mr. Poppinbotham paid her a call. When she had gone to bed the previous night, exhausted from the long journey, she had thought Mr. Poppinbotham might come to her today. But since awakening to the patter of rain upon her windows, she thought not.

That he came in the rain was a pleasant surprise. It was important that she look her best when she went downstairs to see him. She, therefore, took longer than normal on her toilette. Though her selections were limited, she chose a pale green sprigged muslin. When she wore it, she'd been told, it accentuated her pale green eyes. Those making such comments also praised the beauty of her eyes, but she thought they were perhaps just being kind. She pinned back her tresses, and a few tendrils of nondescript brown hair spiraled about her face. She took one last glance into her looking glass, knowing she could not appear to better advantage. That is not to say she looked lovely. She looked tolerable. What a pity that no amount of primping could round out her skinny frame.

Her father had been entertaining Mr. Poppinbotham in the drawing room. Both men rose when she entered. Though the drawing room was normally lovely--owing to her late mother's impeccable taste--it was dreary today, owing to the gray skies and ever-increasing rainfall.

"How lovely you look today, Miss Featherstone," Mr. Poppinbotham said.

"You are much too kind. Pray, be seated." She sat on a faded silken settee close to the fire. Because of the rain, a chill permeated everything, and she was most grateful for the fire's warmth.

"I had hoped to claim you for a ride in the park," Mr. Poppinbotham said, "but, alas, the weather will not oblige."

"Still, I am very happy to see you," she told him. Which was true. Mr. Poppinbotham was integral to her plan.

It was as if her comment added an inch to his stature. A smile settled across his face, and he straightened his spine, while preening like the king of the jungle. The man no doubt fancied that he cut a dashing figure in his striped coat of orange and brown, paired with a waistcoat of lime green. He wore buckled black shoes that would have been far more suitable for a ball than for a morning call. She told herself that when she married him she would have to discreetly assist in the selection of his clothing.

"Tell me again what sent you to Hampshire," he said.

"Lady Wycliff asked me to accompany her whilst they participated in an electioneering meeting for Lord Alex Haversham, who is standing for Blythstone. You will recall he is the brother of the Duke of Fordham." She knew, with Mr. Poppinbotham's adoration of nobles, he would be impressed. She was counting on it.

"A more worthy candidate I cannot imagine," said her father, who had remained as chaperone for propriety.

Mr. Poppinbotham smiled. "How astonishing! I almost met the Duke of Fordham last February. Or was it December? Let me see . . . I was in Bath, and the duke was there also. He drank the waters in the Pump Room. I remember thinking he was such a young man to be a duke."

"Yes," she said, "he was the second son. The first died unexpectedly shortly after succeeding."

Mr. Poppinbotham shook his head. "A pity. But the new duke was most definitely in Bath when I was there. I had hoped for an introduction to him, but alas, it was not to be."

"The man would do you no credit," she said, shaking her head solemnly. "He came to Blythstone, but we were extremely vexed with him."

Mr. Poppinbotham's eyes widened. "Pray, why? "Because the sly devil withdrew his support from his brother, Lord Alex."

"Why did he do that?"

"Because he learned that Lord Alex meant to throw his allegiance to the Whigs."

"Then you are saying the Duke of Fordham is a Tory?" Mr. Poppinbotham lowered his brows in dismay.

A grim expression on her face, she nodded.

"Oh, dear."

Now it was time to invoke her plan. She put her head into her hands.

"What is the matter, my dear Miss Featherstone?" Mr. Poppinbotham asked.

She sniffed. "We are all crushed. Poor Lord Alex cannot proceed against the evil Mr. Hugh Darrington-Chuff without the financial support his wicked brother has withdrawn." She sighed.

"Lady Framptingham--the stalwart Whig that she is--has pledged three hundred toward Lord Alex's campaign, and Lord Wycliff has pledged another two hundred. But Lord Alex still needs a donor with a large purse to ensure victory over his wretched foe. If only we were acquainted with a wealthy man whose heart is in the right place." She once more buried her face in her hands. And sniffed loudly.

"Indeed," her father said, "it is a pity. Quite crushing."

Mr. Poppinbotham left his chair and came to her, settling a gentle hand upon her quivering shoulder. "There, there, my dear Miss Featherstone. You can count on Cecil Poppinbotham to bring wrongs to right."

Her brows drawn together, she peered up at him. "Whatever can you mean, Mr. Poppinbotham?"

"I mean that you *do* know a wealthy man whose heart is in the right place. I feel obliged to support Lord Alex in his plight against that Darrington-Chuff."

She doubted Mr. Poppinbotham knew anything good or bad about the wretched Darrington-Chuff, but she was grateful he would help Lord Alex fight against him. She lifted her face to him, touched his hand, and smiled. "You are our savior, my dear man. You are an angel."

"Indeed you are," her father said. "We are deeply indebted to you, Mr. Poppinbotham. It's imperative that Darrington-Chuff be crushed. He's a thoroughly odious man. Are you acquainted with him?"

Mr. Poppinbotham shook his head. "I do not belong to clubs like White's."

"Perhaps Lord Alex will sponsor his benefactor for membership," she said.

"And who is his benefactor?" Mr. Poppinbotham asked.

"You, my dear man."

Mr. Poppinbotham preened some more. "So I am! Or will be. When I felt obliged to stand for Parliament as a Whig, I knew that it would fall to me to be vastly important to our cause."

"We are incredibly fortunate to have you in our ranks, Mr. Poppinbotham," she said.

* * *

How was she going to tell Lord Slade that Mr. Poppinbotham had offered (with a little push from her) to sponsor Lord Alex's candidacy? Lord Slade had expressly *not* wanted Mr. Poppinbotham's help. He would be angry with her.

She had known since the idea had first germinated that encouraging Mr. Poppinbotham to sponsor Lord Alex would drive a rift between her and Lord Slade. He neither admired Mr. Poppinbotham nor wished to further his connection with the prosperous publisher. But, like Jeremy Bentham promulgated, she must act for the greater good. If she had to forfeit the friendship of Lord Slade over this, so be it--though it would be a source of melancholy to her. Defeating Hugh Darrington-Chuff was more important to more people than a friendship between two people.

Perhaps she could get her father to tell Lord Slade about Mr. Poppinbotham's generosity. Lord Slade would never get angry with Papa. But that would be taking the cowardly way out.

She also considered bypassing Lord Slade entirely and informing Lord Alex that he could proceed with electioneering because he now had a wealthy sponsor. But she couldn't allow Lord Slade to find out second-hand something so important.

Imparting the news face to face with Lord Slade, as distasteful as it was, was the only honorable solution.

* * *

It was to be a perfectly amiable dinner at the Wycliffs'. Unfortunately Alex had sent his regrets. Without the necessary financial backing, he must have decided to bow out of politics before he'd had the opportunity to enter. Slade made a mental note to go see him on the morrow and try to persuade him not to give up. Not yet. A duke's son had excellent prospects. Slade was almost certain help was imminent. Alex had too many attributes not to be a rising Whig star.

As the guests were gathering, Miss Featherstone came up to him. "May I have a private word with you, Lord Slade?"

"Yes, of course." She must wish to impart something pertaining to Lady Sarah. A pity he had not made better progress in his quest to win that lady's heart.

He followed Miss Featherstone to the unoccupied morning room, which was lit by a single taper. She stepped into the chamber but was careful to keep the door open. When she stopped, she turned to face him. Her youthful face was barely illuminated by the soft candlelight which glanced off her chestnut tresses. There was something almost angelic looking about her.

He quirked a brow.

She started to say something, then stopped. Then she drew a breath and spoke barely above a whisper. "I wanted to tell you the good news first."

Good Lord! Had he won Lady Sarah's affections? He could not credit it. "What good news, my dear lady?"

"Lord Alex can proceed with his electioneering. We've found a wealthy man to back his cause."

Somehow, this news was even more welcome than news of the lovely heiress. "Excellent! Who's the man?"

She bit her lip. It made her look like a girl. She did not answer for a moment. Finally, she spoke in a croak. "Mr. Poppinbotham."

He went from bliss to fury in the span of a second. He was so angry he didn't trust himself to speak for a moment, and when he finally did, his voice shook with anger. "You asked him, did you not?"

She nodded solemnly.

"Against my express wishes."

She nodded again. "His money's as good as another man's. What matters is that Lord Alex can proceed. He can defeat that horrid Darrington-Chuff. It's all for the greater good."

"We have no desire to be beholden to that pompous, ignorant, hideously dressed buffoon of a printer." With that, he pivoted, left the chamber, and called out without turning around. "Give my regrets to Lord and Lady Wycliff."

He left the Wycliff's house and strolled aimlessly on foot around the city for hours, unimpeded by the eerily dark streets or the thick, curling fog. After his anger simmered, he felt beastly for the way he'd treated Miss Featherstone when she was only trying to help their cause. Still, she infuriated him. He'd thought he could trust her. She had known he did not want

Poppinbotham's money, yet she had defied him. He would never again trust her.

He--not Miss Featherstone--was to blame for his unnatural animosity toward the Buffoon. Why in the devil did he harbor such ill feelings toward the annoying man? It wasn't because Poppinbotham was such a fish out of water. Slade had never held it against a man that he wasn't born to rank and privilege. Though Slade had found the man to be sadly lacking in knowledge, he had to concede that Poppinbotham must be possessed of shrewd business acumen to have achieved such success in his publishing enterprises.

Slade admired men who wanted to better their lives--and especially if they channeled that desire for betterment to governance for the betterment of mankind. Even though Poppinbotham proclaimed to want to represent the needy masses, Slade was not at all convinced of his sincerity. Poppinbotham wanted to elevate his own stature.

And it was frightfully obvious that while the Buffoon was striving to sit in Parliament, he was also striving to woo Miss Featherstone. She was so far above his touch it sickened Slade to contemplate such an unequal alliance. The man was completely unfit for her. Slade's enmity for the Buffoon had nothing to do with Poppinbotham's class but everything to do with his unwarranted arrogance. His ignorance was matched by his obnoxiousness.

Fortunately, Miss Featherstone was highly intelligent. She was bound to recognize the man's many, many faults, not the least of which was his ignorance of things--like political theory--which she understood with uncommon clarity. There was no way she would ever consider plighting her life to the Buffoon. Even if the man was sinfully rich.

Still, the very notion of the Buffoon courting Miss Featherstone rankled him.

Even though Slade was completely out of charity with her.

He thought long and hard about refusing to take Poppinbotham's money. It rankled him to think he or Alex would ever have to be beholden to a man such as Cecil Poppinbotham. But after hours of wandering through the streets of Mayfair he realized what he had to do.

$\mathcal{C}$hapter 13

It was nearly dawn, but the candles burned brightly in a fine Mayfair house that was Mrs. Nelson's gaming establishment. For reasons incomprehensible to Slade, this is where Alex came when he was feeling low, and Slade suspected that having to withdraw his candidacy must have made his friend low.

He found him at the faro table. Slade's glance whisked to the wager. Five guineas. At least he wasn't beggaring himself with heavy losses--losses he could ill afford. Both Alex's head and his eyelids were dropping. He'd probably been drinking heavily all night.

Slade went to stand beside him.

Alex lazily looked up, then straightened, a querying expression on his face. "What the devil are you doing here?" It was well known that Slade avoided all types of gaming.

"I came to see you. Finish that. We need to talk." And his friend needed to get out of there before he lost far more than he could afford. "Allow me to call for your coach."

"Very well," Alex slurred.

Moments later Mrs. Nelson herself met them at the door as Alex was donning his coat and hat. She'd been a reported beauty some thirty years earlier when, after receiving a settlement from her former lover, the Duke of Argyll, she had bought this house in Mayfair and started her successful business. She was still a handsome enough woman though her midsection had greatly expanded, and her hair was now more gray than brown. "Ah, me dear Lord Alex," she said, curtsying as she bestowed a shimmering smile upon her client, "Lottie and I shall miss you. Pray, don't stay away so long this time."

Slade saw that Lottie of the faro table could not remove her gaze from the handsome duke's son. Alex had never lacked for female attentions.

Alex nodded to Mrs. Nelson. "You can always be assured of my patronage." Then he flicked a glance into the adjoining chamber where Lottie watched him with a somber smile. He nodded then turned back and strode through the open door to his waiting carriage.

"I did not know you stayed awake until dawn these days," Alex said as the coach turned onto Piccadilly.

"You are right. I don't normally. I was going to wait until tomorrow to speak to you on this matter, but since I'd not yet gone to bed I thought now was as good a time as any."

The abundance of brandy Alex consumed had not dimmed his wits. "Then you must have been troubled over this . . . this matter you're going to discuss with me."

"My feelings are irrelevant." Slade shrugged. "I am powerless to even understand my reservations."

"Reservations about what?"

"Apparently, Miss Featherstone had found a wealthy man who seeks to sponsor your candidacy--a man who has become a committed Whig."

"Who is this man?"

Slade knew his friend well enough to know there was something akin to excitement in his voice. So Slade had judged correctly when he surmised that Alex had been disappointed over withdrawing from the election.   "A Mr. Cecil Poppinbotham."

"Is that the fellow who wears the outlandish clothing? The fellow who fancies your Miss Featherstone?"

Linking her with that Buffoon sent Slade's gut plummeting. "She's not *my* Miss Featherstone."

"But I do have the right fellow?"

"Yes."

"It's difficult to believe one such as he could be possessed of a fortune. Are you sure of it?"

"Yes. He started as a printer--printing religious pamphlets. It grew into a very prosperous company. He's even got Hannah More writing for him."

"Then I daresay he's vastly wealthy."

"Rich enough to sponsor his own campaign as well as yours. The more Whigs elected, the merrier." Slade was trying not to interject his own prejudices into this discussion.

"I say, that's awfully decent of the fellow. I suppose now I shall have to sponsor him for membership in Brook's."

"He'd never be voted in. Not unless someone can instill good clothing sense into him."

"There is that. I suppose Miss Featherstone will be able to manage him. Is she not the granddaughter of an earl?"

Slade was so angry over the idea of Miss Featherstone uniting herself to the Buffoon, he felt like lashing out at Alex. "She is," he said through clenched teeth.

"Do you dislike the notion of me accepting aid from this man?"

"It's not my decision. His money's as good as another's, and his is available immediately."

"Then I have no problem accepting it. In fact, I'm grateful to the fellow."

They rode is silence for a moment.

"You still don't keep a coach?" Alex asked.

"Not until I dower and marry off three sisters. Then I might be able to see to my own needs."

"Shall I drop you off at your lodgings?"

"Yes, please."

Slade was dismayed that Alex was quite willing to accept Poppinbotham as his benefactor. He supposed there was nothing wrong with accepting assistance from the Buffoon. After all, having Alex in the House of Commons was the all-important objective even if achieving the objection meant embracing Cecil Poppinbotham.

Why was it no one else was as out of charity with the publisher as he was?

He frowned. He was also out of charity with Miss Featherstone. Never again would he trust her.

* * *

Nothing between her and Lord Slade would ever be the same again. She'd lost his trust. To lubricate his stiffness, she was determined to persuade her cousin to favor Lord Slade. Coaxing Lady Sarah to accompany the earl to Hyde Park would be a way he could be with her without having to compete with her army of admirers. A pity he possessed no coach. A ride in the park was out of the realm of possibility for him, especially now that Jane would not have him share Mr.

Poppinbotham's coach. What about a walk through the park? It was a lovely day, and many people enjoyed walking there on such a day.

With such an aim, Jane walked to Clegg House on Berkley Square. "My, but you're here early," Lady Sarah said.

"I will own I wished to come before the stampede of your suitors."

Lady Sarah rolled her eyes. "The suitors grow tedious."

Jane nodded. "I thought today would be an excellent opportunity for you to get to know Lord Slade better. I believe your array of conversational topics would be expanded by exposure to a man possessed of his vast knowledge--especially of Parliament. It's a subject men know a great deal about, and I believe you will wish to be known as being well informed."

Lady Sarah, who had been examining herself in the cheval glass, turned around, a look of bewilderment on her pretty face. "Yes . . . of course. What do you have in mind?"

"Perhaps a stroll through the park. Green Park is only a moment away. Would you permit me to let his lordship know that you would be amenable to walking with him this afternoon?"

"In place of *holding court* in our drawing room?" Lady Sarah said with a little laugh.

If any other lady referred to presiding over her morning callers as *holding court*, she would sound decidedly vain, but Lady Sarah did not. The beauty had no need to embellish her popularity with opposite gender. "I think so."

"Very well. A walk would be . . . quite novel."

"Then expect Lord Slade to collect you." Jane went to the writing table in her cousin's bedchamber, extracted a piece of velum, and began to pen a note to his lordship.

My Dear Lord Slade,

I have taken the liberty of telling my cousin, Lady Sarah, you would call on her for the purpose of strolling through Green Park with her early this afternoon, and she is most agreeable. If this plan is not agreeable to you, notify me as soon as possible.

Your champion,

Jane Featherstone

It was a significant breech of decorum for an unmarried lady to write to a gentleman, but since this gentleman thought of her only as a *sister*, Jane had no qualms about breaking such a rule. After she stamped the sealing wax with the Clegg family crest, she dispatched one of the Clegg footmen to deliver the letter personally to Lord Slade.

* * *

Miss Jane Featherstone might claim to be his champion, but he was inflexible in forgiving her for going against his wishes. Still, Slade was appreciative of her efforts on his behalf in courting Lady Sarah.

He arrived at Clegg House some time earlier than the hour for paying calls. The butler showed him to the morning room while he delivered Lord Slade's card to the lady. The earl waited no more than ten minutes before Lady Sarah, fetching in pink, swept into the morning room. "Good day, my lord. My cousin appears to have persuaded you that your accompanying me on a walk through the park is exactly what I need to enrich my youthful mind."

He stood, his gaze wandering behind her. Where was Miss Featherstone? Was he to be alone with Lady Sarah? "Is your cousin not coming with us?"

"No. I daresay she does not want my conversation to suffer by comparison to hers. My cousin is uncommonly brilliant, is she not?"

"Yes, she is." He moved and offered his crooked arm to her as they left for their walk.

"Even your brother has commented on her intelligence," she said, looking up at him.

"I daresay he's heard me discuss her on many occasions."

They were the only pedestrians on the pavement of Berkley Square beneath the mid-day sun. "It's a lovely day, is it not?" she asked.

"Indeed it is. I hope we have finally put the rains behind us."

"I do hate rain. I've always said it should only rain at night when we are safely tucked in our beds."

A novel thought--with which he tended to agree. In fact, it was the first time since he'd met her that he found himself agreeing with Lady Sarah. It was a start. He chuckled. "I think that's a brilliant idea. A pity we cannot regulate the weather."

"Indeed it is."

A very fine coach and four was entering the gates to Devonshire House as they walked by. It embarrassed him that he had no carriage with which to carry this lady about Hyde Park.

A moment later they entered Green Park where a great many people were strolling on this sunny afternoon. "Since I have met you, my lord, I am taking a greater interest in reading the newspaper accounts of the goings-on in the House of Commons."

"I'm flattered, my lady. I shall have to quiz you. What is the subject upon which I spoke last week?" He looked down at her. How lovely she was! Her porcelain perfect face was tinged with pink the same soft shade as the dress she wore. Her nose was flawless, and the way her long lashes swept downward was almost seductive. *Almost.* He wished like the devil he *did* find her sensuous. What the deuce was the matter with him? Any other man in the kingdom would be honored to trade places with him right now. But he felt no emotional connection.

She did not answer him for a moment. She looked rather like a recalcitrant child who'd been caught with its hand in the plum pudding. "La, my lord! I confess I only look for your name because you're so important a personage, and I feel so privileged to know you."

He inwardly cringed. The girl had not enough interest in her own government to read a single article in the newspaper. He tried to act flippantly. "Were you afraid your father would see you reading about an infamous Whig?"

She laughed. "Perhaps I was. Papa cares not for Whigs--except for Uncle Featherstone, with whom he wildly disagrees."

"But one can never dislike Mr. Featherstone. He's much too admirable."

"He's the kindest of men."

"That, my lady, is why he is a Whig. He cares for people. He's opposed to slavery. He advocates better wages for workers. He opposes working children. All these things anger rich men who profit from other people's oppression."

Her eyes widened. "If you're speaking of my father, I'll have you know he has never owned slaves!"

"Forgive me if you thought I was referring to your father. I was not."

"But you're a nobleman. How can you turn your back on your own people?"

He did not answer for a moment. "Perhaps if you would read the works of Jeremy Bentham you would get a sense that we must put aside our own needs and desires to work for the greater good."

"Do you have such a book you could lend me?"

It was a start. "I would be happy to."

They went to Buckingham House and came back to Piccadilly. Twice they walked the perimeter of the park, then he escorted her back to Clegg House. "My cousin said walking with you would improve my ability to converse more intelligently. I do believe she was right. I thank you, my lord, for coming to me today."

As he walked back to his lodgings, he felt grateful to Miss Featherstone for initiating today's walk. It had been a huge step toward bringing him and Lady Sarah together. If she would only take the effort to learn about political philosophy, he was sure he could fall in love with her.

Chapter 14

During the following week Slade saw neither Lady Sarah nor Miss Featherstone. He was, therefore, looking forward to seeing Miss Featherstone at the Wycliffs' dinner this evening-- not because he necessarily wanted to see her but because he was anxious to learn if Lady Sarah had read the Jeremy Bentham book he'd sent her several days earlier.

To his delight, Alex attended the dinner and sat at Wycliff's right. Just after the soup was finished, Wycliff got everyone's attention. "It is my pleasure to announce that Lord Alex Haversham will be able to proceed with his campaign to defeat Hugh Darrington-Chuff. Another Whig candidate who's standing for Plymouth has provided the rest of the monies needed for Lord Alex's candidacy."

"Who is the generous man?" Lord Babbington asked.

"A Mr. Cecil Poppinbotham," Alex responded. The smile on Alex's face and the enthusiasm in his voice gladdened Slade.

Lord Smythington lowered his bushy brown. "Poppinbottom? Never heard of the fellow."

"It's Poppinbotham," Mr. Featherstone said. "He's a prosperous publisher of religious pamphlets."

"Jolly good," Lord Aylesbury said.

Slade was happy to see that Lady

Framptingham had become the third lady in attendance--in addition to Lady Wycliff and Miss Featherstone--at this dinner. He had not only come to admire her but also to consider her a powerful Whig advocate.

"'Tis very glad I am that Lord Alex can continue his campaign," that lady said. "I can almost smell his victory. The last gathering in the shire's to be next week. With flowing taps and pressing the flesh from our Whig candidate, who happens to be the son of a duke, I'm certain Lord Alex will win."

Her husband beamed at his wife. "I daresay he'll soundly beat that odious Darrington-Chuff."

"I hope you're right," Lord Alex said.

If Alex's enthusiasm carried over to his position in the House of Commons, Slade knew he'd be an extremely capable Parliamentarian. But, as Slade had cautioned Poppinbotham, they must not take victory for granted.

He had no opportunity to speak to Miss Featherstone during the dinner, as she was seated at the center of the table, and he was at Lady Wycliff's left. Toward the end of the evening's festivities, he made it a point to approach her as she and her father were gathering their cloaks. He was disappointed that things would never again be the same between them since she had defied him. "Pray, Miss Featherstone," he said, touching her shoulder, "I beg a quick word with you. In private."

She glanced at him, then at her father, who nodded. She and Slade ducked into the library, where the chamber was illuminated from the fire blazing in the hearth. They stood some little distance inside the door, and she looked up at him. The expression on her face was completely different from that during any of their previous tête-à-têtes. Was it fear? His gut clenched. Had his berating of her destroyed the camaraderie they had always known? In spite of his former anger with her, he felt like a pariah.

"I wished to ask you if you know if Lady Sarah has read the Jeremy Bentham I sent."

She hesitated a moment before responding. "I saw it in her bedchamber and questioned her about it just this afternoon. Though my cousin expressed great interest in reading it, she has yet to pick it up." Miss Featherstone drew a breath. "I should warn you that my cousin is not enamored of reading. I once urged her to read Thomas Paine, but I regret to say she has yet to do so. She means well, but her mind does not run to the things that mine or yours do."

"So you're telling me I would do best not to try to change her?"

"I am. You must accept her as the lovely being she is."

He nodded.

"I can tell you she plans on going to Almack's on Wednesday."

"Will Poppinbotham be taking you and her?" he asked.

"Yes, actually. Were you not so ill disposed toward Mr. Poppinbotham, it would be to your advantage to accompany us."

"I have made up my mind to suppress my ill feelings toward Mr. Poppinbotham. After all, he's been exceedingly generous to my dear friend." He paused a moment. It was difficult for him to say what he was going to say, but he must be magnanimous. "And, my dear Miss Featherstone, I would be sadly remiss if I did not thank you for your efforts on my behalf with Lady Sarah. The walk in the park was a brilliant plan, and I believe it strengthened my connection with your cousin. I know it did on my part."

"You're very welcome. It was the least I could do since I'd ignited such anger in you."

He knew he should apologize, but her defection was still too raw. He merely nodded and guided her from the chamber.

With the departure of the Featherstones, he was at liberty to speak with Alex about next week's electioneering near Blythstone. "I will miss the vote on the Civil List, but I do plan on accompanying you on your next electioneering visit. I promised I'd always come, and perhaps I can lend my voice if the need should arise."

"It's not necessary, Sinjin. You're needed for the Civil List vote." Alex clapped a hand around Slade's shoulder. "I must stand on my own two feet. I don't want the voters to think you're my nursemaid."

Instead of being offended that he wasn't needed, Slade was exceedingly proud of his friend. He stood back and gazed at Alex, admiration shining in his eyes. "I knew you would be a great Parliamentarian."

* * *

On Wednesday Slade subjected himself to both Poppinbotham and Almack's. The things one must do for one's family. He danced precisely four dances, two with Lady Sarah and two with Miss Featherstone. Fortunately, when he wasn't dancing he was not subjected to having to converse with Poppinbotham. That man actually made a cake of himself dancing with every lady who would do him the honor. He even claimed to enjoy dancing. Slade believed he enjoyed most hanging onto the coattails of the nobility.

Midway through the evening, Alex strolled into Almack's large assembly room. The matchmaking mamas in the chamber all took note of the handsome duke's son, the son next in line to a vast dukedom.

It was difficult for Slade to evaluate another man's handsomeness, but he believed women found Alex highly desirable. Not that Alex had any interest in settling down. He enjoyed his life--and his many dalliances--just the way it was.

The two old friends stood along the room's perimeter and talked. "Who is that lovely blonde in ivory?" he asked, his eye darting to Lady Sarah.

"That is the lady I escorted here tonight."

Alex gave him a quizzing look. "I've never known you to be enamored of beauties. Not bright enough for you."

"This one is also an heiress, and I'm in desperate need."

"Then I shall not ask her loveliness to dance."

"Thank you." Slade didn't think he stood a chance if Alex was in the running for the lovely lady's hand. Alex could charm women in ways of which Slade was completely ignorant. What he'd said about Slade was true. Slade had never been in the petticoat line. And he probably didn't stand a ghost of a chance with the beautiful heiress.

But he was hell bent on trying.

They stood and watched Lady Sarah for a moment. She had danced every set that night.

"Why are you here?" Slade asked. "I didn't think debutantes appealed to you."

"They don't, but my sister's supposed to be here, and I promised I'd ensure she was not a wallflower."

"Lady Margaret?"

"Yes."

Slade smiled. "She will never be a wallflower."

Alex shrugged. "But she failed to get an offer last season."

"It's intimidating to think of asking for the hand of a duke's daughter. One must be at least the rank of an earl, and there aren't that many bachelor earls around."

"There is no such rule. She's free to marry any man she chooses."

"But the men feel as if they're not good enough for her."

"We did experience something similar with Kathryn. Remember, it took her three seasons before she had an offer."

"And it's a good thing she waited. Roxbury's a fine fellow."

"Yes, they don't come any finer."

"Are you going to dance?"

Alex eyed Miss Featherstone, who was dancing with Poppinbotham. "I see Miss Featherstone is dancing with my benefactor. I believe I shall ask her to be my partner the next set."

The only part of the evening Slade enjoyed was when Alex was there to amuse him, but once his sister and her group arrived, he transferred his attentions to them. Slade felt badly his own sisters had yet to be presented. Hopefully, the eldest could come out next year. Even if he didn't succeed in securing the hand of Lady Sarah, he should be able to squeeze out enough money to launch Mary Ann.

* * *

Alex's sister Margaret was, indeed, exceedingly

courteous to consent to stand up with the most hideously dressed man at Almack's: her brother's benefactor. Someone must instruct the man how to dress.

Dancing with the daughter of a duke gave Poppinbotham a great deal of satisfaction. He talked of nothing else when they got into the carriage later that evening.

When Slade could stand it no longer, he addressed Miss Featherstone on a different topic. "Tell me, Miss Featherstone, when will I be able to persuade you to sketch Dunvale Castle?"

"I would be happy to do it tomorrow, your lordship, were I able to observe it, but it's a bit difficult, given that Dunvale is in Kent, and we're in London."

"Ah, but my good Miss Featherstone, Dunvale is scarcely over an hour's drive from London--once one gets past the city's crush. I shall have to contrive to take you there."

"I should love it above all things," she said. "It would be lovely for Lady Sarah and me to breathe country air for a few days, would it not, Sarah?"

"Oh, indeed it would."

"And I should be honored to offer my coach and four," Mr. Poppinbotham said proudly.

In all the kingdom, Slade could think of no other man who could be a more annoying companion than Mr. Poppinbotham, but he must be beholden to the man for the use of his carriage. "That would, indeed, be very kind of you." He turned to Lady Sarah. "My sisters will be thrilled beyond comprehension to meet you and your cousin."

"And I should be delighted to meet them, my lord," Lady Sarah said. "If they are half as agreeable as you and your brother, I know we will get on famously."

"Shall we set a date?" he asked.

"I could wrap up my pressing business in two days," Mr. Poppinbotham said. "How about Saturday?"

"Saturday it will be then."

Chapter 15

The next two days could be the most important in his life. He would have Lady Sarah to himself with no intrusion from her adoring masses. He hoped that the deep bond he so strived for would have the opportunity to form between them. Surely he would be able to fall in love with a lady of such beauty–and wealth. Hopefully, when she saw him in his role as lord of the castle, she could fall in love with him, too. His softer side would certainly be on display in his interaction with his sisters. Perhaps that would appeal to the lady.

If he could just see to it that her exploration of the castle did not extend beyond the lone occupied wing that was furnished with the finest pieces from the Slade holdings. A person could break a leg–or worse–if he or she ventured beyond that one stable wing.

As he and Poppinbotham rode in that gentleman's carriage to collect the cousins on Saturday, Lord Slade felt oppressed. There was no turning back from this path, this quest for the heiress's hand. Adding to his oppression was the fact he must keep company with the Buffoon. The man set his nerves on edge.

"Well, my lord, this could be a momentous journey for Cecil Poppinbotham."

Lord Slade's gaze whisked over his traveling companion. The man had outdone himself this day with his attire. It was as if he were trying to see how many different colours he could attempt to coordinate. There was the brown of his, admittedly fine, leather boots. His breeches were of buff. Then the colour began to pop. Cutaway coat of lime green with exceedingly large mother-of-pearl buttons paired with an orange shirt and turquoise waistcoat. The chief offender was the man's cravat. It. Was. Black! There was the advantage that spilled food would not be that noticeable on it, but if he thought to start a new trend in men's clothing, the poor fellow was in for grave disappointment. "Why do you say that, Poppinbotham?"

"I have decided to honor Miss Jane Featherstone by asking her to become my wife."

Had the man just confessed to murdering the Princess of Wales, Slade's reaction could not have held more contempt. The arrogant creature thought a marriage proposal from the likes of him was an honor! The very notion made Slade sick. It was all he could do not to send a fist crashing into the pompous man's face.

But that wouldn't do.

Slade sat there, staring at the Buffoon as if he were an alien creature, and all the while he was attempting to gather his thoughts, to compose a response that would in some way display the good breeding his mother had attempted to instill in him. Though he fairly well shook with anger, he managed to still the quiver in his voice long enough to say, "Is this not rather sudden?" Which was much less offensive than the first ten responses which raced into Slade's head and ranged from, "You bloody, bloody, idiot" to "How dare you think you're fit to marry a lady with Miss

Featherstone's many attributes!"

"I've never been one to beat about the bush, no sir, or should I say, no, your lordship? Never let it be said that Cecil Poppinbotham let grass grow under his feet. I know what I want, and I'm not afraid to go after it. I didn't get where I am today," his self-satisfied gaze swept over the plush interior of his elegant carriage and settled on his bright green coat, "by waiting for opportunities to drop in me lap."

"I would hardly call Miss Featherstone an *opportunity.*"

When the carriage pulled up in front of Featherstone House, the conversation came to an end.

But Lord Slade's accelerating heart rate did not.

***

When he had ridden to Almack's with Lady Sarah seated beside him, Lord Slade had found the accommodation agreeable. But for the two-hour ride to Dunvale, he could not like having to stare across the carriage at the Buffoon seated so close to–and so possessively attentive of–Miss Featherstone. It was enough to steal Lord Slade's appetite.

As they advanced through London's busy streets, he tried to tell himself Mr. Poppinbotham's choice in a wife was nothing to him. But the more he thought on it–and, admittedly, he seemed incapable of thinking of anything else–the more repulsed he became by the notion of Miss Featherstone uniting with Cecil Poppinbotham.

Then it suddenly occurred to him that Miss Featherstone would never stoop to accept the pompous printer. True, the man's wealth could be attractive to some women, especially to one who came from a family that didn't have a feather to fly with. But since Miss Featherstone was possessed of extraordinary intelligence, she could never be expected to suffer a fool.

Marriage, as he was himself being forcefully reminded during this journey, was a lifetime commitment. Miss Featherstone was much too wise to sentence herself for life to a man in want of good judgment.

Having rationalized himself into a good humor, he faced the lovely blonde seated beside him. "I am bereft of words to tell you how excited my sisters are that you and your cousin are coming."

"I must own," that lady said, "I am looking forward to meeting them. Pray, you must tell me their names and ages."

"Mary Ann is the eldest. I believe she's the same age as you."

"And she hasn't been presented?"

"It seemed wiser, in the light of other considerations, to wait until next year."

"And your other sisters?" Lady Sarah asked.

"Remarkably, the three of them are spaced exactly a year and a half apart. The middle sister, Diana, is sixteen, and Lizzie, the youngest, is fourteen and a half and wishes she were seventeen."

Lady Sarah's face brightened. "Tell me, my lord, will Captain St. John be at Dunvale?"

"Indeed he will. He rode over yesterday and plans to stay there the duration of our visit."

"He is so very pleasant to be around," Lady Sarah said.

"Just don't get him started talking about India,

or you'll never hear of anything else."

"But I find India vastly interesting."

"Yes," Miss Featherstone added, "there's something so exotic about that land."

"But who'd want to live among all those dark-skinned creatures?" Mr. Poppinbotham asked.

The earl glared across the carriage. "My brother has made many friends who have dark skin. I pray you don't speak like that in his presence."

"Oh, but your lordship, I meant no offense."

Once they left London's sooty skies behind them, Lord Slade opened the curtain on his side of the carriage. The vision of verdant meadows, reposing sheep, and clear blue skies overhead was enough to lift his spirits. He did enjoy going to the country.

A pity he wasn't going to someone else's country house. He had never loved Dunvale as his father had. For him, it had always represented decay and never-ending repairs that drained every cent in the family coffers.

"I find myself wondering if the natives can read English," Mr. Poppinbotham said. "If I could get my religious tracts and pamphlets circulated in a country as large as India, I'd have enough money to buy. . . Windsor Castle!"

Was money the only thing Poppinbotham ever spoke of? Lord Slade glared again. "I don't think Windsor Castle will ever be for sale."

"And I'm not altogether sure the natives can read or write in their native tongue, much less in English," Miss Featherstone added. "Though I'm sure those of the higher classes–a small number, I am told–are quite well educated."

"Glad I am that you've brought up illiteracy," Mr. Poppinbotham said, "for compulsory education is one of those matters you, my dear Miss Featherstone, told me I needed to acquaint myself with before I sit in Parliament."

"It is definitely one that a progressive man like yourself needs to embrace," she said.

How sly Miss Featherstone was! She was attempting to mold the Buffoon to her own progressive agenda. "So, as a progressive, Mr. Poppinbotham, I assume you favor compulsory education?"

"When I get in Parliament, I will most certainly promulgate opportunities for all Englishmen, regardless of their class, to learn how to read and write, and I assure you such a cause has never been motivated by the vast profit such a movement could be to my own publishing enterprises."

"How very commendable," Slade said.

"Surely you don't think even a chimney sweep needs to be taught to read?" an incredulous Lady Sarah asked, her mouth gaping open.

"I certainly do. Every child in the kingdom should have the opportunity to read Scripture," Poppinbotham answered.

"Well," said Lady Sarah, "I sponsor a Sunday school back at Stockton-on-Wye, but I think it a ridiculous extravagance to want to educate every child in the kingdom."

"You have been listening to your papa," Miss Featherstone said good naturedly.

Her intervention prevented Slade from saying something harsh to the woman he needed to marry.

A pity he could not think of Lady Sarah as the woman he *wanted* to marry.

$\mathcal{C}$hapter 16

When she first beheld Dunvale Castle rising above the pastoral countryside of rolling hills in the mid-day sun, Miss Featherstone's thoughts flashed to knights of yore and maidens in wide silken skirts and headdresses snugly fitted over coiled tresses. It was a quintessentially English castle constructed of gray stone with turrets protruding from the corners of its crenellated roofline. Not terribly large, as castles go, but formidable and solid.

Like the present lord of the castle.

Her gaze flashed to Lord Slade. In his chocolate brown coat, buff breeches, and finely tanned boots, he was the very picture of masculinity. She could still feel the brush of his lips against her cheek all those days ago. She had been unable to purge him from her mind. Not since the night he had kissed her. Even though it wasn't a proper kiss and even though, to him, it was but a brotherly kiss, it was the only time a man had ever kissed her.

Nothing had ever so moved her. Joy had sung through her veins. Then reality had set in, and she was filled with a sense of profound loss. For the only man she could ever love was going to marry her cousin.

And Jane Featherstone would likely spend the rest of her life attached to a man whose kisses would never affect her as Lord Slade's had.

"Look at Dunvale, Sarah!" Miss Featherstone knew how much her cousin adored castles. That Lord Slade possessed a medieval castle would undoubtedly be one of the strongest recommendations for plighting her life to his.

The lady flicked open her curtain and peered at Dunvale Castle, wonderment sparkling in her sapphire eyes. "It's just what a proper castle should look like!" She turned to the man seated beside her. "Does it have a moat?"

"Not for the past two hundred years," his lordship said ruefully.

The lovely blonde smiled at him. "Well, I cannot tell you how excited I am that I'll actually be spending the night in a real castle."

"I am very happy to hear that," Lord Slade said. "Dunvale's very different from what it was in medieval times. During the last century we added outbuildings and formal gardens *outside* of the castle walls. My father was especially proud of the garden he had designed by Capability Brown, even if it was one of Mr. Brown's smallest projects."

"Then I daresay," Miss Featherstone interjected, "we shall find man-made waterways at Dunvale."

Lord Slade met her gaze, amusement flashing in his dark eyes. "Indeed you will. I see you know the hallmarks of a Capability Brown landscape."

"As you know, my lord, architecture—even landscape architecture—holds great interest for me."

"I hope you brought your drawing supplies," he said.

"Indeed I did, my lord."

Mr. Poppinbotham brushed up against her as he attempted to peer at their destination. "I declare, that's quite a fortress you've got there, my lord. Daresay it would set a man back a fortune to acquire something so grand."

Money again. Miss Featherstone gritted her teeth. Is that the only thing the man could discuss?

"I daresay it wouldn't matter how deep the buyer's pockets, it's not likely a castle that's not a complete ruin would ever come on the market." Lord Slade spoke as if he were talking to a child. "They're always in the entail, and even when there's no heir, they revert to the crown."

"I do know of several men of wealth who have built new castles," Miss Featherstone said. "And while Lord Cowper's Panshanger is not new and was never built as a castle, in his latest creation of it, he's added features that make it resemble a castle."

"I shouldn't at all like a mock castle," said Lady Sarah, scrunching up her perfect nose, "not when one could have something as alluring as Dunvale Castle."

The coach wheels rattled over the drawbridge, the castle's huge timber doors opening up for them as they rolled into the spacious bricked courtyard before stopping at an arched door. "I hope Dunvale Castle doesn't disappoint," Lord Slade said as the coachman assisted them from the carriage.

***

Lady Sarah's reaction to the castle was all Slade had hoped it would be. "Oh, look, the ceilings are so very high," she had exclaimed as soon as they entered the great room. "Has Dunvale truly been here ever since the Conquest?"

He nodded.

The lady then raced to the fireplace. "I declare, my lord, even a man as tall as you could stand here! It's frightfully massive."

At least she had noticed he was possessed of height above that of the average man. He was never really sure she paid the least shred of attention to him.

Like a toddler running in the fields, she flew from one feature to the next, snapping off questions and barely having the patience to wait for an response. *Do you have suits of armor? How many hundreds of years since it was built? Look at the size of these stones!*

She strolled from the great room and stopped dead in her stride as she gazed at the wide stone staircase. "Oh, look! One can almost picture an entire regiment of soldiers in suits of armor marching abreast up these."

A moment later, she said, "Pray, my lord, where will my chambers be?" She seemed incapable of removing her gaze from the broad steps that had worn smooth over the centuries.

Perhaps her attention had been captured by the large celestial tapestry which hung high on the curved stone wall there. He'd been told it was one of the most valuable possessions at Dunvale. "Actually, I'm not exactly certain where your chambers will be, my lady. My sisters will have made that determination. I daresay the rooms will be in the family wing, which is a laborious climb three floors up."

"I shan't at all mind climbing these stairs. I feel as if I could be at King Arthur's court."

He chuckled just as his brother entered the chamber. Must David always wear his uniform? He looked entirely too much like the handsome hero of a romantic tale, the kind of tale he was certain Lady Sarah would enjoy.

"How good it is to welcome all of you to our home," Captain St. John said. He looked first at Miss Featherstone and bowed, then his eyes met Lady Sarah's and held.

Lord Slade facilitated the introductions between his brother and Poppinbotham, and minutes later repeated introductions when his sisters entered the huge, cold chamber.

"If I met you on Conduit Street," Lady Sarah said to the eldest of the three sisters, "I would immediately take you for sister to Captain St. John and Lord Slade. The family resemblance is very strong."

"I pray I look more feminine," Lady Mary Ann said with a laugh.

"Oh, indeed, you do. You're not at all tall, like your brothers, and you're exceedingly pretty." Then Lady Sarah turned her attention to the other sisters. "But I must own, the two of you look nothing like the others."

Lord Slade squashed his hand on top Lizzie's head and spoke good naturedly. "We always say Lizzie's the runt of the litter."

"Just wait," Lizzie challenged, "I'll catch up with my sisters."

"I'm afraid, Pet," said the middle sister, Lady Diana, who was the only blonde in the family, "that may not happen. You're fourteen now. Mary Ann and I were fully grown by the time we were your age."

"It's amazing to me how different the three of you are," Miss Featherstone said. Her gaze flicked to their eldest brother. "You must be very proud of your lovely sisters."

He nodded as his gaze fanned over his sisters. "I hope I do not flatter myself that as each of them is presented, they will receive many offers of marriage. Not that I ever wish to be rid of them."

"Put that in the betting book at White's, and you could make some blunt," Captain St. John said.

Lord Slade's lips curved into a smile. "No I could not. No man would be foolish enough to take the bet."

Mr. Poppinbotham loudly cleared his throat. "Glad I am that I've no sisters I have to dower."

Money again. The crass man had broached the one subject Slade wished to avoid. Even though Lady Sarah was bound to know he needed to marry an heiress, he hated to be obvious about it. Every lady should believe a man courted her for herself, not her money. He stiffened. "Oh, but Poppinbotham, I could never regret these delightful creatures."

Captain St. John put his arm around Lizzie. "Nor could I. It's great fun having younger sisters to tease."

"How fortunate all of you are to have grown up in a real castle," Lady Sarah said. "All my life I've adored castles."

"Has my brother shown you the priest's hole?" Captain St. John asked the lady.

Her hands flew to her dimpled cheeks as a sunny smile brightened her face. "You have a priest's hole at Dunvale?"

"Indeed we do," David answered, holding out his hand. "Allow me to show it to you."

The two of them disappeared around the corner.

A pity Lady Sarah was always so shy in his own

presence. He wished she adopted with him the easy camaraderie she and David shared. Those two got along quite like an affectionate brother and sister, which, he supposed, was a good thing, seeing as how they would be brother and sister if his plan succeeded.

Good manners dictated that Slade offer to show the priest hole to his other guests. "Should you care to see it, Miss Featherstone? Mr. Poppinbotham?"

"I should love to," Miss Featherstone said.

"Pray, my lord," Poppinbotham said, "you must explain to me about these priest holes. Am I to understand you–or your ancestors–shoved priests down a hole?"

Slade chuckled. "Ours isn't a proper hole, as you'll see, but, yes, my ancestors most certainly did hide priests after the Dissolution."

When they reached the dining room, David was demonstrating how to open the priest's hole. David, who had always been fascinated by Dunvale's priest hole, tapped at the movable panel in the center of the wood-paneled wall, and one of a series of vertical oak boards opened as if it were on hinges. The space behind the board was actually a small, windowless stone room. The opening was so narrow, a large man like Slade would not be able to squeeze into the secret chamber.

An excited Lady Sarah raced through the opening, giggling like a child. "So this is where the priests used to hide! How vastly interesting."

"It is said our ancestor, Sir Matthew St. John, defied Henry VIII and kept his Papist faith," Slade explained when she came back out.

"Indeed," David expanded, "it was not until the

third generation into the Tudor regime– after the baronetcy had turned into an earldom–that the Slade family fully embraced the Church of England."

As they spent the afternoon exploring the castle, it occurred to Slade that his brother's interest in the ancestral pile far exceeded his own. A pity David hadn't been the first born.

Chapter 17

At sweet Miss Featherstone's request, Slade allowed Lizzie to sit at the dinner table that evening. His youngest sister took her place at the table between Miss Featherstone and Diana. "I am very indebted to you," Lizzie said to Miss Featherstone, "for asking that I be allowed to dine with you. Are you aware that this is the first time I've ever sat here?"

If he was not mistaken, Miss Featherstone often wore the same mint green dress as she wore tonight. Though it was limp and faded, it was not unbecoming on her.

"I was not, but I hope that every time you sit here over the course of your life, you will remember with affection our stay here."

"Oh, you may be sure of it!" Lizzie glanced across the table and addressed Lady Sarah. "And I shall always remember that you were not only the prettiest lady I've ever seen but also the most fashionably dressed."

"Indeed," Diana said, her own covetous gaze whisking over the lady's elegant lavender gown. "It is exciting for hermits like us to see a reigning London beauty who has such an eye for all that is fashionable."

"La! Lady Diana, you shall put me to the blush." He could have liked a bit more modesty in his prospective wife. Lady Sarah easily accepted lavish compliments and adoration as her due.

Those at the table busied themselves filling their plates with sturgeon and French beans and passing the bowls of pickled beets and creamed potatoes.

He could not have been more pleased over the dinner. He did not know how she had contrived it, but Mary Ann had seen to it that the normally gloomy chamber was so brightly lit. It nearly looked like daytime from four braces of candelabras on the long table.

He never failed to admire the Slade family china which bore the family's heavily gilded stag crest.

"I understand, Mr. Poppinbotham," Lady Mary Ann said, "that you plan to stand for Parliament." Leave it to his most serious-minded sister to steer conversation back to matters other than fashion and beauty.

"Indeed I do . . ." He turned to Miss Featherstone, who sat next to him. "Miss Featherstone is attempting to educate me. This lady is possessed of uncommon intelligence as well as an extraordinary breadth of knowledge on political theory." His attention returned to Lady Mary Ann. "And your estimable brother has been invaluable."

"Then I daresay my brother's got you reading Rousseau," Mary Ann mused.

The Buffoon shrugged. "I shall need to compile a reading list."

"One cannot read Rousseau and not Voltaire," Lord Slade said.

Miss Featherstone set a hand to Poppinbotham's sleeve. "And you must read John Paine."

How remarkable that she would recommend

Paine. "My own political philosophy was more influenced by Paine than by any other writer," Lord Slade said.

Miss Featherstone turned toward him. "Then, my lord, I daresay you must admire Edmund Burke's writings."

It was remarkable how much Miss Featherstone's thinking mirrored his own. "I cannot praise the man highly enough." He turned to Poppinbotham. "I urge you to read him, too."

"How fortunate I am to have your lordship offer such sage guidance."

Lord Slade shrugged, then made eye contact with Miss Featherstone again. "As you know, I believe your father is the best orator in the House of Commons today. Listening to him is one of my greatest pleasures. One of my greatest regrets, though, is that I never got to hear Burke."

She favored him with a smile. "It's the very same with me, my lord! Papa cannot speak highly enough of Mr. Burke's abilities as a speaker who used such perfect logic--though he did not always agree with him."

He nodded. "I understand he and Charles James Fox were two of the finest speakers ever on the floor of House of Commons."

Mary Ann addressed him. "I remember how excited you were that time you came down from Eton just to hear an oration by Charles James Fox. You were barely seventeen."

"I'm very glad I did." His lips folded into a grim line. "Within a year he was dead."

"My father was completely distraught over his death," Miss Featherstone added.

"I beg you not to talk of death or politics anymore," Lady Sarah said, turning her attention to David. "You must tell us of your adventures in India, Captain St. John."

David shrugged. "I fear, my lady, that my sisters would attempt to strangle me were I to accommodate your request."

"Indeed," Diana said. "We have heard the same stories scores of times."

David addressed Lady Sarah once more. "Perhaps tomorrow you will do me the goodness of allowing me to share some of my tales from India."

"I should love it above all things," she said, smiling shyly at him.

"Then after breakfast, I'll take you for a walk outside the castle grounds."

Mary Ann, a natural hostess, redirected the conversation, this time asking Mr. Poppinbotham about his business.

* * *

After dinner Miss Featherstone played the pianoforte in the more intimate drawing room where the cold stone floors were covered with thick Turkey carpets, the windows were draped in red velvet, and a fire blazed in the more modestly sized hearth. Despite that it was in a castle, this room had a comforting quality. She thought that could also be attributed to the blocks of dark wood paneling which sheathed the walls. The wood was so dark from age it had turned almost black.

She had quickly seized a seat in front of the instrument so she would not be called upon to sing. If one hundred ladies were to sing this evening, Miss Featherstone had no doubts she would be the worst of the lot. Because her physical attributes were greatly lacking, Miss Featherstone was possessed of just enough pride that she never wished her other defects displayed.

Lady Sarah, as the guest, sang first. Her voice perfectly matched her angelic looks. What man would not fall in love with her? How Miss Featherstone envied her cousin her many blessings. And now a new one could be added. Soon, Lady Sarah would acquire three sisters! All their lives she and Sarah had lamented they had no sisters. Did Sarah have to get everything? Could there not be a crumb left for her poor relation?

Then Miss Featherstone would feel wretchedly guilty over her jealousy. She loved Sarah and always wanted what was best for her cousin, just as Sarah wanted what was best for Jane. They had always looked upon each other as sisters.

When Lord Slade saw that Miss Featherstone was having difficulty turning the pages of the music while playing the pianoforte, he came and sat on the bench beside her and began to flip the pages for her. She recalled him telling her that he was a great music lover.

Instead of comforting her, though, his close proximity sent her heart racing and her hands trembling. Whatever was the matter with her? Miss Jane Featherstone had never been so profoundly affected by a man before. If only poor Mr. Poppinbotham could elicit such a reaction in her!

After each of the ladies had sung–with Miss Featherstone politely declining–Lord Slade turned to Mr. Poppinbotham. "Would you care to sing for us?"

"Oh, dear me, no. Never had time for music."

Of course he didn't. No money to be made there, Miss Featherstone thought, most uncharitably. "But my dear Mr. Poppinbotham, you've spent four decades toiling to make your fortune; now it's time to indulge in life's pleasures," she said, "and music is most definitely one of those pleasures."

He offered her an appreciative smile. "'Tis blessed I am to have met the likes of you, Miss Featherstone. You not only understand me perfectly, but you know exactly what I need for the next rung on the ladder of success."

"You are a fortunate man, indeed," Lord Slade said.

Jane felt wretchedly guilty for any uncharitable thoughts she had toward the printer, er, publisher. "Tell me, Mr. Poppinbotham, do you know how to play the pianoforte?"

He shrugged. "I'm embarrassed to admit it, but I do not."

Miss Featherstone addressed him. "There's nothing to be ashamed of. You paid handsomely for a dancing master to teach you to dance, and I can vouch for his success. Why do you not engage someone to teach you the pianoforte? That is, if you are inclined to *want* to play at the pianoforte. You are obviously an apt pupil."

The flattered man tossed a glance to their host. "You must see, my lord, how very good Miss Featherstone is for me."

She thought perhaps Lord Slade was losing his patience with the other man. He was barely civil when he said, "Indeed I do."

* * *

It was nearly midnight when the sisters showed Jane and Lady Sarah to their bedchambers on the third floor. Lady Mary Ann, holding high a brace of candles, led the way. "This is the family corridor," she said. They began to pad down the broad wooden hallway where the only source of light was a lantern sconce midway down the hall.

"How many bedchambers on this corridor?" Lady Sarah asked.

Jane could tell her cousin was clearly impressed over the monumental size of Dunvale's interior. Lord Clegg's country home was a great deal smaller.

Lady Mary Ann set an index finger to her chin. "Let me think."

"Twelve," Lizzie announced proudly.

"The rooms we're putting you ladies in are almost identical. The only difference is Lady Sarah's is emerald coloured, and Miss Featherstone's is in red." Mary Ann stopped in front of a tall timber door and opened it.

Since the room was green, Jane knew it was her cousin's.

Lady Sarah hurried into the chamber where a fire glowed from the small hearth, and emerald coloured broadloom carpet covered the cold stone floors. The bed was draped in velvet the same shade of green as the carpet. The occupant was elated. "What a wonderfully cozy room! Who would have thought a castle could be cozy?"

"I'm glad you like it," a clearly delighted Lady Mary Ann said.

"Oh, I assure you, I love Dunvale," Lady Sarah said.

"We are so gratified. I hope you sleep well, Lady Sarah." Mary Ann faced Jane. "Now to your chamber, Miss Featherstone."

The fire in Jane's bedchamber had also been laid. She hoped these few days at Dunvale were not costing his lordship an excessive amount he could ill afford to spend. She had noticed at dinner that dozens of costly wax candles lighted the long oaken dining table. Such an expense!

"Thank you, Lady Mary Ann." Jane turned to the other sister. "I am decidedly appreciative that you've made mine and my cousin's stay here so comforting and enjoyable." She – as well as her cousin – had taken an immediate liking to the sisters. They displayed a genuine warmth of character and well-informed minds. Just like their eldest brother.

"The joy is all ours," Lady Diana said.

"Indeed, it is a delight to have guests," Lady Mary Ann added.

Lizzie smiled. "Tomorrow we shall steal you away from the males and bombard you with questions about the newest fashions in London and the assemblies at Almack's."

"You're much too young to be filling your head with such things," Lady Mary Ann chided as she set a gentle hand on her sister's shoulder and guided her from the room.

"My cousin will be happy to discourse on fashion," Jane said. "It is a subject upon which her knowledge is vast."

"I could certainly tell that by the quality of her beautiful clothing," Lady Diana said.

Lady Mary Ann sighed. "As if one that lovely even needed beautiful clothing!"

Alone in her scarlet bedchamber, Jane put on her night clothes, then climbed onto the high bed that on colder nights would be enclosed with the scarlet velvet draperies that now gathered around the four bedposts. She lay there in the semidarkness, the wood fire crackling in the grate, her thoughts spinning over the day's events, then settling on Mr. Poppinbotham. Until today, she had not admired the man, and while he had yet to do something to earn her respect, tonight he had won her affection.

Certainly not the same kind of affection which Lord Slade elicited in her, but now she saw Mr. Poppinbotham as a man struggling to better himself. And he needed her in order to accomplish what he wished to accomplish in life. The very notion of being needed gave her a sense of purpose.

She tried to imagine being kissed by Mr. Poppinbotham, but the thought made her exceedingly uncomfortable. Not like with Lord Slade. The very idea of kissing him had a profound physical effect upon her entire person–a pleasant physical effect. Indeed, she could think of nothing which could be more pleasant.

She had come to believe that Mr. Poppinbotham meant to ask for her hand in marriage. She was flattered that among all the pretty ladies surrounding them this evening he only had eyes for her. Would he ask for her hand in marriage on the morrow? What would be her response?

$\mathcal{C}$hapter 18

"Whatever is the matter, Runt?" Lord Slade asked Lizzie as he entered the saloon the following morning and saw her reddened, teary eyes.

"My . . . my persecutor insists that I cannot get out of my lessons today." She glared at her eldest sister.

He stopped and regarded Mary Ann. "I appreciate that you have Lizzie's best interest at heart, and I'm cognizant that it's a great burden having to serve as mother and father while I'm away, but I think this once it can't hurt for her to take a day away from lessons." He knew how much Lizzie loved a picnic.

Mary Ann's features softened. "Honestly, Slade! You are such a tender heart. I knew you'd come right behind me and undermine my efforts to instill self discipline in her."

He drilled Mary Ann with a stern look. "Can you honestly tell me Lizzie is so deficient in knowledge that she cannot miss a single day of instruction?"

"You know she's more than capable. She's too devilishly clever, by far." She mumbled under her breath. "She's entirely too much like you."

He hugged Mary Ann. "A most fortunate girl, to be sure."

Lizzie flew to him and threw her arms around him. "You are the best brother any girl ever had."

"Indeed you are, Slade." Mary Ann looked up at him with admiration shining in her eyes. "It's you who have all the burdens. It's not fair that you're saddled with all of us, and you're not yet thirty."

He stiffened. "Pray, don't ever speak like that. I count myself as the most fortunate man in the three kingdoms to have four such delightful siblings."

"All the same," Mary Ann said, "it's a pity you had to make that Vow."

He shrugged.

Mary Ann pushed at Lizzie. "Go tell your governess you'll not be taking lessons today."

After Lizzie left the chamber, and the two of them were alone, she spoke her mind. "I know that wretched Vow is forcing you to dance attendance upon that empty-headed – albeit beautiful – heiress when it's plain as the nose on your face that Miss Featherstone's the very girl for you."

He felt rather as if someone had walloped his chest. Miss Featherstone! He had never given the lady the slightest consideration–in a romantic way.

Because he knew he could not.

He had a duty to his dying father. His own preferences were not to be considered. There were too many people dependent upon him. "You are quite mistaken. Have you not noticed that Miss Featherstone and Mr. Poppinbotham are courting? I believe the man means to propose to her during their stay here at Dunvale."

She winced. "That would be a terrible shame."

"Why do you say that?"

"They are so mismatched." She nibbled at her lip, then lowered her voice. "And because I know she's in love with you."

"You can certainly know no such thing!"

"But I do, Slade. Women know about these things."

He looked at her skeptically. "Seventeen is hardly a woman."

"You've told me all my life I'm much older and wiser than my years. It's because I'm the firstborn daughter with the attendant responsibilities, just as you, as the firstborn son, have even greater responsibilities."

"You understand I have to court Lady Sarah."

She solemnly shook her head. "I just wish you had free will to marry the woman who would make you the best life partner."

He turned away, then spun back and faced his wise sister whose face so resembled his and David's–in a pretty version. "What makes you think Miss Featherstone has the least interest in me?"

She lowered her voice. "Surely you can't believe her serious about that hanger-on!"

"Actually, no. I am sure Miss Featherstone has more sense than that." He continued to lower his voice because he really would not want poor Mr. Poppinbotham to hear him. He certainly did not dislike the man. It was just that he was so far beneath the touch of the impeccable Miss Featherstone.

Mary Ann shrugged and kept her voice low. "I can't actually say how I know Miss Featherstone's in love with you. Perhaps it's the way she watches you. Or the way she looks so sad when you communicate with her cousin. Or perhaps it's the way she seems to perk up like a pup whenever you address her. Certainly nothing like she responds to her so-called suitor." Mary Ann abruptly stopped talking, her gaze darting to the doorway.

He turned and saw Miss Featherstone. "Good morning," he said, bowing. "I have good news. The dark clouds have gone, and we will be free to take our country walk and to have our picnic this afternoon."

"That is good news," Miss Featherstone said.

"Where's your cousin?" he asked.

"Your brother has stolen away with her. She consented to allow him to regale her with tales of India."

"Are they in the library?"

"No, I believe they're walking outside the castle grounds."

He had wanted to be the one to show her the parkland surrounding Dunvale. He'd always thought it Dunvale's best feature.

"This morning I should love to ride," Miss Featherstone said. Was she trying to take his mind off his disappointment?

He frowned. "I'm afraid we don't keep a proper stable here at Dunvale."

Her face fell. "Oh, of course. You do spend most of your time in London, but - - -" She suddenly must have realized he kept no stable in London, either.

Poppinbotham entered the chamber, chatting amiably with Diana. The man's face brightened when he saw Miss Featherstone.

Lord Slade did not at all like to think of Miss Featherstone encouraging the poor man. Not when there was no way an intelligent woman like her—a woman from one of England's oldest families, no less—would even consider uniting herself to someone like Cecil Poppinbotham.

Perhaps Slade should have a word with her today, let her know of Poppinbotham's plans so she could give the best consideration as to how to let the old fellow down gently.

* * *

David led the way along the broad lawn to the rear of Dunvale, Mary Ann on his left, and Diana on his right. Next came Lord Slade, with Lady Sarah linking her arm to his and an adoring Lizzie strolling beside the Paragon of Fashion and quizzing her unmercifully about London fashions. Miss Featherstone and Mr. Poppinbotham were just a few feet behind them.

"Have you decided what angle you wish me to use when I sketch Dunvale, my lord?" Miss Featherstone asked.

It was as if she'd stolen into his thoughts for he had been wondering the very same thing. "Ideally, I'd like to get the lake in the foreground."

She laughed. "I was going to suggest the same thing. You know, my lord, I was a bit surprised when you expressed in interest in having me draw Dunvale."

His step slowed, and he turned to look back at the lady. He hated to address anyone– especially a lady–when his back was presented to her. "Why do you say that?"

She shrugged. He noticed that, unlike her cousin who wore a lovely pink velvet pelisse on this cool day, Miss Featherstone wore a knitted shawl of dark green--practical and economical, like the lady who wore it. The green shawl was perfectly becoming on her. "It's just that I never felt you held Dunvale in great admiration," she said.

He gave a bitter laugh. "How very well you know me, Miss Featherstone. I must own that one of the reasons I wished to have a good drawing of Dunvale was to have it for my brother when he's off on his travels for crown and country. My brother seems to have inherited all the affection for the old pile that the heir was supposed to possess."

"I have noticed that Captain St. John does seem every bit as enamored of the castle as my cousin," Miss Featherstone said.

"I declare, Cousin Jane, I believe you're right!" Lady Sarah gave a scolding look up at her escort. "Really, my lord, you should be more proud of your ancestral home."

He sighed. "But my dear lady, I've taken the liberty of sparing you exposure to Dunvale's warts."

She looked straight ahead. "I shouldn't think there could be any warts at Dunvale that could not be repaired with a hefty purse."

"But alas, my lady, I'm sadly in want of that." As uncomfortable as the confession made him, he was relieved that he'd finally been honest with the young lady. He was also relieved to have all his warts out in the open. He disliked deception of any kind.

As they continued on, with Lizzie and Lady Sarah discussing fashion, he pondered what the lady had just said. *There couldn't be any warts at Dunvale that could not be repaired with a hefty purse.* Surely that had to mean she was considering him as a potential husband. Isn't that exactly what he wanted?

Then why did he feel so very low?

The land surrounding the castle resembled a

green carpet that was symmetrically dissected by a wide gravel path. As they strolled across its vast expanse, pockets of trees stood out in the distance. These had been carefully planted to provide as many varying shades of green as possible. Though Lord Slade looked upon the castle itself as a burden as well as a cold and grim monstrosity of a building, he enjoyed its landscape.

Once they neared the trees, Capability Brown's curving lake came into view. Lord Slade always smiled when he noted the little humpback stone bridge that spanned the lake at one of its narrower points. That had been his mother's lone contribution to the landscape.

"I declare, my lord," Lady Sarah said, "one could never want to return to London."

"I cannot convey to you how happy those words make me."

They circled the lake, and then still farther beyond they came to the summer house, a neoclassical structure situated on a manmade hill that overlooked the lake. There, his footmen were setting up tables for their picnic while Cook and the scullery maid were unpacking baskets that were brimming with food and drink.

By the time their group reached the summer house, they had walked for an hour. House was an inaccurate name for the structure. It was really more of a pavilion because it had no proper walls. Doric columns supported the pedimented roof.

Several tables had been laid out to make one long table that was now generously set with food. There was cold mutton, fresh country cheese, apples, hard-cooked eggs, and ale and wine with which to wash down the meal.

"Please feel free to sit where you'd like," Slade said.

Lady Sarah ended up with a brother on either side of her. As the meal progressed, Lord Slade was disappointed in himself for not being a more interesting conversationalist. David, on the other hand, practically held court. He had Lady Sarah listening in raptures to his tales of India. What a pity that he, Lord Slade, was incapable of establishing a closeness between himself and the young lady he was trying to woo.

He had hoped he and Lady Sarah could stray from the others today in order to establish some intimacy between them, but most of his thoughts were being channeled into the question of how he would find the opportunity to prepare Miss Featherstone for the inevitable question Poppinbotham intended to present to her. Slade did not at all like to allow Poppinbotham to speak to her before he himself had a chance to warn the young lady.

While David was telling Lady Sarah about some raja's palace, Lord Slade found himself watching Miss Featherstone across the table. How attentive Mr. Poppinbotham was, insisting on serving her and soliciting her opinion on food preferences. Then once the man realized his host was not engaged in conversation, he began to quiz him.

"I say, my lord, while Miss Featherstone is drawing your castle this afternoon, I thought I'd like to poke about in your library."

"You are certainly welcome to borrow any book you choose."

"Have you the writings of this Thomas Paine?"

"Indeed, I do. I will be happy to find it for you when we return to the castle." Lord Slade met

Miss Featherstone's gaze. "I hope you'll allow me to help you bring out your chair or anything else the artist might need."

`She looked a bit puzzled for a moment. She was aware he had footmen who could provide such a service, but she was her gracious self when she replied, "That would be very kind of you, my lord. Perhaps you will be able to show me from which angle you'd like me to draw Dunvale."

"You're the artist, my dear Miss Featherstone, but I will endeavor to convey my preferences."

* * *

He found *The Rights of Man* for Poppinbotham while Miss Featherstone raced upstairs to fetch her drawing supplies, then the two were ready to go back outdoors. She carried her sketchbook while he toted one of the folding chairs they had used at the picnic.

"I have very much enjoyed my stay at Dunvale, my lord. And I must tell you your sisters are a delight. I feel a special affinity for Lady Mary Ann. It's almost as if we've known each other all our lives."

"She told me she's very fond of you." He laughed. "She even thinks I should wed you!" The woman strolling beside him stiffened at his words. "Forgive me for laughing," he said. "Of course, Mary Ann has good reason to think you'd make me a fine wife. I even agree with her, but you and I know such a thing is not possible."

She nodded. "Most certainly."

They strolled across the vast stretch of lawn in silence. When they reached the lake, she took some time getting her perspective. When she decided on it, he set up her chair, and she settled down and began to sketch.

He cleared his throat.

She looked up at him. "Yes?"

"I hoped to have a private word with you today."

She continued to look up at him with those solemn green eyes. They were very fine, very expressive eyes. "About what?"

"About Poppinbotham."

"I see."

"I'm not really sure you do. Are you aware that the man means to ask for your hand in marriage?"

Her brows lifted. "Has he told you so?"

"Yes."

"I must admit that your announcement is not unexpected."

"It was really too mean of you to lead on the poor chap. Just because he's not one of us doesn't mean he doesn't have feelings. In fact, I believe he's not only wanting to marry you to help his social climb. I believe the man has really come to care for you."

"Yes, I had reached quite the same opinion."

"How can you just sit there looking up at me so innocently? I beg you to consider the poor man's feelings."

"Oh, I assure you I have, my lord."

Her words gave him pause. "Whatever can you mean?"

"I mean that I am not averse to plighting my life to Mr. Poppinbotham."

He felt as if he'd just been knocked off his feet by a cyclone. His gaze locked with hers, a sizzling anger rising in him. "You cannot possibly be in love with the man!"

Her lashes lowered. "No, I cannot."

He dropped down to his knees before her and

drew her hands into his, "Then for God's sake, Jane, don't throw yourself away on him." He suddenly realized he'd called her by her Christian name. In his nine and twenty years, he had never slipped in such a manner. At least not with a proper lady.

Tears gathered in her eyes, but she made no effort to swipe them away. It fairly broke his heart to see her suffer. Almost as much as it broke his heart to think of her lying beside Cecil Poppinbotham.

"You must understand, my lord, Mr. Poppinbotham is the only man who has ever fallen in love with me. That I am poor and plain should not relegate me to a spinster's life. I should like my own home, my own children. Mr. Poppinbotham can give me those things. And I assure you, he is exceedingly kind to me."

A surge of powerful emotions stampeded him. She was neither plain nor unloved! By God, a man would be a fool not to love her.

Jack St. John, the Earl of Slade, had never done a rash thing in his life. Until he drew Miss Featherstone's upper torso into his arms and began to kiss her with a hunger which bowled him over with its intensity.

Just as surprising as his action was the lady's reaction. She kissed him with the kind of passion he would have thought a spinster like her incapable of. God in heaven, but she felt so sweet in his arms!

But unlike Mr. Cecil Poppinbotham, Lord Slade was not at liberty to ask for her hand in marriage.

Because of that wretched Vow.

With a deep, gnawing ache, he pulled away from the most perfect female he'd ever known.

"Forgive me, Miss Featherstone. I had no right."
Then he got to his feet and strode away.

* * *

Somehow during the next few minutes Jane
managed to continue sketching his lordship's
home even though tears raced down her cheeks.
Why did Lord Slade have to go and spoil
everything? She had convinced herself that
marrying Mr. Poppinbotham would be very good
for her.

Even if the thought of kissing him was not.

Why had Lord Slade felt compelled to kiss her?
She had never thought him a man who would
casually toy with any maiden's affections. He was
always the very picture of propriety. Everything
about the scene between them a few minutes
earlier seemed like something she had dreamed,
something that had no basis in reality.

And, indeed, she had best relegate the memory
of it to the same place where abandoned dreams
resided.

Her heartbeat roared. Now that she had been
properly kissed by a man with whom she was in
love, how could she ever submit to Mr.
Poppinbotham's kisses? The very memory of his
lordship's kiss made her insides feel like quivering
jelly. How wondrous the kiss had been! Dare she
even think. . .he desired her in the same way she
had always desired him?

Because of her wanton response to him, Lord
Slade was bound to think her a harlot. How could
she ever face him again after that searing kiss?

Even worse, how could she ever consider
spending her life with a man whom she could
never kiss as she had just kissed Lord Slade?

$\mathcal{C}$hapter 19

Were it not for the friendly banter between Captain St. John and Lady Sarah, dinner would have been a grievously somber occasion. Their host had glowered from the head of the table. Even after the meal when they gathered in the drawing room, his lordship hardly spoke.

More than once she had caught him staring at her, but Jane was always quick to look away. She had been embarrassed over the unexpected intimacy between them. She prayed he would not think her a loose woman, prayed that his good opinion of her–which she knew with certainty she had possessed *before* the kiss–would not change.

She was far too intelligent to confuse his good opinion of her with romantic interest. They were two entirely different matters. For reasons she could not understand, something had compelled the earl to kiss her. Even had he not begged her forgiveness, she knew he immediately regretted the action.

Now they both must forget it. He needed to marry an heiress, and she needed to accept Mr. Poppinbotham because she was quite certain this was her only hope of marrying and becoming a respected matron and mother.

For despite what had occurred between Lord Slade and her, she was going to accept Mr. Poppinbotham. She must.

* * *

Slade might be sitting at the head of the dinner table, but he was certainly not presiding over the table. No one could have been a worse host. No one else could feel as forlorn has he did that night. He could not bring himself to offer a single comment. Since he'd been overcome with the incredible yearning to kiss Jane Featherstone, he felt his life--and that of his loved ones--in shambles.

What had possessed him to act so contrary to everything he had ever believed? He'd believed he would never question his duty. His duty was to save Dunvale because he had promised his father. His duty was to see three sisters properly dowered. That latter duty he could do by depriving himself of certain things that could be had with money, but no amount of economizing would ever net enough funds for Dunvale. Marrying an heiress was the only way that could be accomplished. And that would most certainly deprive him of true love.

He now knew he could never proclaim himself in love with Lady Sarah. He'd given that other vow to Jane Featherstone that he wouldn't propose to Lady Sarah unless he could declare himself in love with her.

And he could never tell such a monstrous lie.

All afternoon, Jane had dominated his every thought. Jane and the passionate kiss that had consumed them both like a raging wildfire. The very memory of it caused his breath to hitch, caused his body to ache with the need to hold her once more in his arms.

Slade's haunted gaze fell on her when she passed Poppinbotham the stewed eel and spoke in her sweet voice to the Buffoon. Something inside Slade exploded. He suddenly realized he was in love with Jane. Truly. Madly. Deeply.

And there was nothing he would ever be able to do about it.

When the stewed eel reached him, he passed it on. Each dish he passed on. He moved the small bit of food on his plate around and around but was incapable of eating.

Near the end of the meal the door to the dining chamber swung open with a great deal of noise. All eyes went to the doorway where Alex had come to a stop, his booted legs planted, his eyes glittering, and a teasing smile on his face.

Now Slade spoke. "What the devil brings you here?"

"I was compelled to share my good fortune with one of my dearest friends--as well as with my benefactor." Alex eyed Poppinbotham.

"Pray," Slade said, "what is your good fortune?"

"I've won."

Poppinbotham's eyes widened. "You beat that Darrington-Chuff?"

A smile stretching all the way across his face, Alex nodded. "Indeed. With the money you so kindly supplied, Mr. Poppinbotham, I was able to woo far more voters than I needed, and I'm happy to say many of them were defectors from Darrington-Chuff's camp."

Finally, something for which to cheer. A wide smile on his face, Slade stood, crossed the room, and heartily shook his old friend's hand. "This is wondrous news indeed." He turned back to his guests. "This calls for celebration."

David leapt to his feet. "I'll show the footmen where Papa stored his best champagne."

"An excellent idea," Slade said. How was it David always knew more about Dunvale and its contents than he did?

Moments later, the champagne had been poured and glasses lifted. "I offer a toast," Slade began, "to my dear friend Lord Alex who will be one of the finest Parliamentarians Britain has ever known."

A smiling David shook his head in protest, but everyone else chugged down the champagne.

"Another round," Slade ordered.

When another round of glasses were filled, he said--even though it stung to praise the man who would marry the woman Slade loved, "To Cecil Poppinbotham for his willingness to learn about and support all Whig causes with his great generosity."

Poppinbotham was not as modest as Alex had been. He drank to his own toast and not once shook his head.

"You must come partake of food with us," Slade said to Alex.

"I cannot. As you see, I'm still in my boots."

Slade shrugged. "It matters not. We're almost finished, and you must be famished. Have you come all the way from Blythstone?"

"I have." Alex did move to the side chair a footman had wedged between Slade and Diana. Another footman set a plate in front of him, and he began to pile it with food that had lamentably grown cold.

"I wish Wycliff were here to celebrate with us," Slade said. "It will be just like it used to be at Eton. The three of us together, the three of us always working in unison."

"And," Jane said, peering at him, "I believe this

time it will be even more rewarding."

Slade's gaze connected with hers. Neither could look away. His gut plummeted. He trembled. He nodded.

Then he looked away.

* * *

Before they retired for the night, Mr. Poppinbotham addressed her. "I beg, Miss Featherstone, that you will do me the honor in the morning of walking to the lake with me."

Her heartbeat drummed. She knew the purpose of their solitary walk. "I should be honored, Mr. Poppinbotham." Before she turned away and began to climb the stairs, she saw that Lord Slade was watching her.

And listening.

That night she closed the heavy velvet curtains tightly around her bed, and then she lay there in the total darkness. Even the thick curtains could not keep out the night's morose sounds. Winds howled. Rain fell in lusty sheets. And the logs in her fire spit, crackled, and collapsed time after time.

While she wept.

She hadn't wept since her mother died when she was a little girl. Tonight she felt that same, horrifying sense of loss. It was entirely too cruel that on the verge of committing herself to a man who would wed her, she had a taste of what it was like to be with the man she loved, the man she could never marry. She had always known that Lord Slade was far, far above her touch.

And nothing had changed.

Except the kiss.

Now she would unite herself to a man she did not love. Never again would she experience a shattering kiss like she'd experienced that day.

$\mathcal{C}$hapter 20

The rains stopped at dawn, and a few hours later, a bright sun appeared. If she wore boots instead of slippers, Jane supposed she could still walk with Mr. Poppinbotham this morning. They must have a care to stay on the lawns and avoid any dirt paths which were sure to be quagmires of mud.

She donned her warmest woolen dress for it had become chilly, and she selected her red cloak to wear when they departed after breakfast. Though she made every effort to contrive to fashion her hair attractively, she knew she failed. She stared into the mirror at her dowdy reflection and lamented that she was no beauty like her cousin. *I am very lucky that one man in the kingdom wishes to honor me with a proposal of marriage.*

She would never have another chance.

As she descended the stairs, her thoughts raced ahead so fast, she could barely isolate one when another cropped up. The worst part about accepting Mr. Poppinbotham was going to be announcing the decision to Papa. He did not perceive that his cherished only daughter failed to attract men. And, of course, he would have wished for her to marry a man who was more of their world, a man more well read than the prosperous businessman who wished to claim her hand.

But she was of age. She did not need her father's approval to marry.

Telling Papa was *not* the worst thing about accepting Mr. Poppinbotham. Resigning herself to a life without romantic love was worse. She wondered what it would feel like to have a man like Lord Slade wish to marry her.

Lamentably, with that thought in mind, she faced Mr. Poppinbotham as she entered the morning room, where they gathered for breakfast.

Once again, Lady Sarah–fetching in pale blue muslin–was talking and laughing with Captain St. John, and once again, Lord Slade brooded. How distressing it must be to him that the lady he wished to marry was more comfortable with his brother than with him.

Throughout breakfast she avoided looking at Mr. Poppinbotham. It was not the poor man's fault that his appearance did not please her. She kept schooling herself to regard him as the well-intentioned man who wished to honor her with his name and fortune. *I must not be disappointed that he is not handsome. Nor should I be disappointed that his intelligence is not great.* The man was possessed of many fine qualities. He was a hard worker who had built his own fortune, which was a lot more than she could say about any other man of her acquaintance. He was serious about bettering his station in life. He was neither afraid to admit when his knowledge was lacking, nor was he averse to asking for advice. A most admirable quality, to be sure. Above all, as she had told his lordship, he was exceedingly kind to her.

She smiled to herself. Her Papa would at least be gratified over that.

After breakfast, with assistance from Mr.

Poppinbotham, she donned her cloak. "I am happy to see you've worn boots today, Miss Featherstone. I daresay it's muddy out there. And cool, too."

She slipped her arm through his. "Yes, it was a very cold night."

They left the castle keep, crossed the courtyard, walked over the wooden planks of the former drawbridge, and soon they were strolling along the grass which squished beneath their feet from the relentless rains of the previous night.

"Did the foul weather impede your sleep?" he asked.

"Yes." That and other things. "I hardly closed my eyes all night."

He patted her hand. "I am distressed to hear that, but I admit, it was the same with me."

The touch of his hand was nothing like the touch of Lord Slade's hand. Oh, the devil take it! She must quit thinking about Lord Slade, must drive thoughts of their kissing and touching from her mind. Forever.

For some unaccountable reason, she did not wish for silence. If they kept up casual conversation, she could postpone the regretted inevitable, that inevitable proposal she must accept.

"How are you liking Dunvale Castle, Mr. Poppinbotham?"

"I keep pinching myself to see that Cecil Poppinbotham is really the guest in a castle owned by an earl! If only my dear mother were alive so as I could tell her."

Jane laughed. Mr. Poppinbotham might be forty, but in some ways he could be refreshingly childlike.

"Tell me, how is your drawing of the castle progressing?"

How could she tell him she had not been able to draw for more than a few minutes because Lord Slade's kiss had so completely shattered her? "I, um, couldn't seem to get the right perspective. Perhaps I can try again this afternoon."

"When we get back to London, you shall have to show me your architectural drawings. I had no notion of how many talents you possess, my dear Miss Featherstone."

"You are much too kind."

"I have a great respect for artistic abilities. I have the devil of a time getting qualified artists to illustrate my pamphlets."

It crossed her mind to lightly ask if he would hire a woman like her to draw for his business, but she knew if she brought up her lack of financial prospects, he would be quick with an offer of financial security for life--as his wife.

And she wished to prolong facing the disappointing inevitable.

Eventually they found themselves well on the other side of the lake, so far from the castle that it was completely out of view. "Come, Miss Featherstone, and sit on that bench with me. There is something I wish to . . . to discuss with you."

Her heartbeat roared and clanged. Her hands grew moist and trembled.

Pulling her skirts beneath her, she sat on the sturdy wooden bench. He came to sit beside her, and he drew her hand within his. "My dear Miss Featherstone, for some time now I have been - - -"

A great pounding sound interrupted him, and they both spun around to see what the noise was.

Lord Slade, atop a galloping stallion, was racing toward them.

Her eyes widened. Whatever was his lordship doing?

He brought the horse right up to the bench, leapt off, and faced her, his dark eyes blazing with emotion. Was it anger? "I beg you not to accept this man's proposal."

What in the blazes? "But, my lord, he has not proposed."

"Good." Lord Slade then dropped to his knees, not having the least care that he was muddying his superfine breeches. "Forgive me, Poppinbotham, but I must attempt to claim Miss Featherstone for my own wife."

Jane's mouth gaped open. Surely her ears were deceiving her! "But, my lord, you cannot marry me. I have nothing to offer."

"Oh, but you do," Lord Slade said. "It is my most ardent desire that you consent to become my wife. No other woman will ever do for me."

"But, what about your Vow?"

He drew her hand into his and pressed a soft kiss atop it. "I have given the matter considerable thought and have decided it's far better to break my word to a man who's dead than to ruin the lives of four, possibly five, who are living."

"What can you mean?" she asked.

"It would be cruel to marry another woman when I can only ever love you, Jane. It will break my heart irrevocably if you wed Poppinbotham, and it wouldn't be fair to wed him when you're in love with me."

So her response to his kiss the day before had betrayed her.

Mr. Poppinbotham's mouth gaped open. "Is this

true, Miss Featherstone?"

These past two days she was turning into a complete watering pot! Her eyes once again filled with tears. Then she began to heave great sobs while nodding in agreement with wonderful Lord Slade.

Mr. Poppinbotham mumbled a curse beneath his breath, got to his feet, and began to stalk away. "Then I shall be leaving Dunvale immediately. I trust you'll be able to manage your return journey to London without my coach and four!"

She felt ashamed of herself for having led him on, but otherwise, her heart was brimming with joy.

His lordship spoke in a husky voice. "You, my dearest love, haven't given me your answer."

She continued sobbing. "I know I should refuse because marriage to me cannot answer your needs- - -"

He pressed gentle fingers to her lips. "Never say that. You are the only woman in the kingdom who can answer *all* my needs."

Then he pulled her into his arms and thoroughly kissed her.

She wasn't sure how it happened, but she ended up kneeling beside her dearest Jack, the skirts of her dress becoming soaked with mud. Nothing had ever felt so good as being held in her darling's arms. Nothing could ever make her happier than his declaration of love. "My dearest, dearest Jack, I love you far too much to refuse your most welcome offer."

Then they kissed again. For one with little experience at kissing, she thought she had taken to it better than any new thing she'd ever learned.

Finally he stood and offered her a hand. She looked at him with searching eyes. "Dearest?"

"Yes, my love?"

"To whom were you referring when you said four, possibly five lives, could be ruined if we married the wrong people?"

"Besides you and me and Poppinbotham?'

"Yes, you goose."

"Lady Sarah or whichever woman I would have wed for fortune. I assure you, I could never love anyone but you, Jane."

Her tears stung again. "And the possible fifth?"

"I believe my brother may be falling in love with Lady Sarah."

She was not altogether sure her cousin wasn't falling in love with the dashing captain, too. None of Sarah's many admirers captured her attention as much as Captain St. John. "Perhaps if you gave him the castle, Lady Sarah would be eager to marry him. She is most enamored of medieval fortresses."

"By Jove! That sounds like a capital plan."

"You must know my needs are simple. I would be as a kitten in a sunny window in the merest room of a cottage, if I could be with you."

"Would that we were in such a room right now. Would you object if I procure a special license to marry immediately?"

She giggled. "Nothing could make me happier."

There was a lightness in his voice and in his step. "I cannot believe how happy you've made me."

"It is the very same for me, my dearest, dearest Jack."

They joined hands and began to walk back to the castle. "Allow me to add a sixth," she said.

His brows dipped. "A sixth what?"

"A sixth person who will rejoice over our nuptials--my papa. I know he will think you are exactly what I need. Dear papa always believed any man--even a handsome peer of the realm like you--would be happy to win the hand of his beloved daughter."

Her darling Jack dropped one more kiss upon the crown of her head. "You are exactly what I need."

&pilogue

Two weeks later

He was the happiest of men. Lord Slade stood before the altar at St. George's Hanover Square with his cherished bride beside him, their hands clasped. Making the day equally as special was the couple standing beside him and his dear Jane. He glanced to his right to observe David, handsome in his regimentals, standing happily with his bride, Lady Sarah. Two brothers marrying two cousins.

He keenly felt the presence of all his loved ones. His sisters sat in the front pew, and his father's presence was almost palpable. He knew his father would be happy to know that David's wife was going to see that Dunvale Castle was preserved. Indeed, David and Lady Sarah were planning to live there, planning to raise their family there.

Slade and Jane would be happiest in London, where they could be near Parliament--and close to Jane's aging father. Lord Slade was not a wealthy man, but now that Lady Sarah had offered to present–and to dower—her new sisters, he and Jane would be able to live comfortably.

His Vow to his father was being honored.

Now the priest was asking him to make another Vow. *"Wilt thou have this woman to thy wedded wife, to live together after God's ordinance in the holy estate of Matrimony? Wilt thou love her,*

comfort her, honor, and keep her in sickness and in
health; and, forsaking all other, keep thee only unto
her, so long as ye both shall live?"

Lord Slade turned to Jane, and his heart overflowed with his sacred love of her. "I will."

This was one Vow that would be his pleasure to honor. For as long as he lived.

The End

The Lords of Eton series

This book is the second in my *The Lords of Eton* series about three aristocratic lads who were best friends at Eton and how their escapades and interests continue to tie them--and the women they love--together after Eton.

The first book in the series is *The Portrait of Lady Wycliff,* loosely based on my out-of-print book *The Earl's Bargain.* The third book will be *Last Duke Standing,* scheduled for publication in late 2018.

Author's Biography

A former journalist and English teacher, Cheryl Bolen sold her first book to Harlequin Historical in 1997. That book, *A Duke Deceived*, was a finalist for the Holt Medallion for Best First Book, and it netted her the title Notable New Author. Since then she has published more than 20 books with Kensington/Zebra, Love Inspired Historical and was Montlake launch author for Kindle Serials. As an independent author, she has broken into the top 5 on the *New York Times* and top 20 on the *USA Today* best-seller lists.

Her 2005 book *One Golden Ring* won the Holt Medallion for Best Historical, and her 2011 gothic historical *My Lord Wicked* was awarded Best Historical in the International Digital Awards, the same year one of her Christmas novellas was chosen as Best Historical Novella by Hearts Through History. Her books have been finalists for other awards, including the Daphne du Maurier, and have been translated into eight languages.

She invites readers to www.CherylBolen.com, or her blog, www.cherylsregencyramblings.wordpress.co or Facebook at https://www.facebook.com/pages/Cheryl-Bolen-Books/146842652076424.